THE SEVENTH
COLOUR OF THE
RAINBOW

SEVENTH COLOUR
OF THE
RAINBOW

UNA J BRYAN

JANUS PUBLISHING COMPANY
London, England

First published in Great Britain 1996
by Janus Publishing Company
Edinburgh House, 19 Nassau Street
London W1N 7RE

Copyright © Una J. Bryan 1996

British Library Cataloguing-in-Publication Data.
A catalogue record for this book is available
from the British Library.

ISBN 1 85756 255 0

Cover design Linda Wade

Printed and bound in Great Britain by
Antony Rowe Ltd, Chippenham, Wiltshire

The characters and situations in this book are entirely imaginary
and bear no relation to any real person or actual events.

For my sister Joan,
with thanks for her love and compassion

Prologue

The youth, sitting beside a stream signed his name and date – W A-J 1936 – in the corner of his painting. Placing it beside him, he watched the weeping branches of a mutepe tree tease the gently flowing water. After a while he glanced down at his painting – the work had dried. Protecting the picture in a folder, he gathered his belongings and emerged from the seclusion. Crossing a ploughed field, he walked along an avenue of saplings. The young trees were planted a few years ago on his mother's insistence. Slowly, he followed the road to the sprawling mansion in the distance. At the sound of a vehicle behind him the lad stepped aside. The car stopped beside him.

'You are William Jones, I'm a friend of your father's,' said the driver as he pushed back his hat to reveal a partially receding hairline.

'William Auston-Jones,' corrected the youth.

'Yes Auston-Jones, I forgot. Auston was your mother's maiden name.' The driver smiled and pointed to the folder in the youth's hand. 'What have you there?'

William opened the folder and showed the man the watercolour.

'That's excellent. I'll tell your mother to have it framed and hung in the house. Is your father at home?'

'He's at the stables with my sister.'

The driver thanked William and went on his way.

Chapter 1

The pioneers, a small gathering of weary men and women stood around the flag-pole. They placed their hands on their hearts, sang the national anthem and pledged allegiance to the Motherland across the sea. Without any more pomp or formality the ceremonial flag was raised to symbolise the birth of a new colony, another jewel for the Imperial crown. The birth of the colony had been difficult, for the pioneers laboured many weeks in pain and misery and overcame both human and natural adversities to achieve their ambitions. They became a nation that survived its allotted time, three score years and ten.

Through the subsequent years the pioneers faced many more difficulties, yet tenaciously they held on, tamed the land and buried their dead under the msasa tree. As the colony prospered, misleading reports of fortune and wealth reached the southern parts of the continent. These accounts, false as they were, encouraged others to make the long trek to the north.

Misplaced people, visionaries, missionaries, a miscreant or two decided to search for their fortunes. They gathered their belongings, formed a column and chose a leader.

'Which way must we go?' they asked a seasoned explorer.

'North, and keep the east coast on the right and the mountain range on your left,' he suggested. 'Cross the Limpopo River but not the Equator. The place you're seeking is somewhere there.'

The adventurers began their journey. Travelling to the east

for many weeks, they turned northwards keeping close to the foothills of the jagged mountains.

With heavy wooden yokes across their necks the oxen, bred to endure the hardship of semi-desert and scrubland, hauled the wagons over the veld. The 'voor-lopers', small boys, barefooted and in ragged clothes, led the docile, faithful animals.

Each might before sunset the pioneers formed a laager and the families gathered around the camp-fire for warmth and safety. In the light of the flames, the wagons circled the sleepers like grotesque insects guarding their young against the African night. Close by in the make-shift kraal the scrub oxen pawed the ground and snorted their hot breath into the cold morning air.

Before the break of the false dawn, the boys rose to inspan the beasts. They pushed and pulled the animals into line and placed the heavy yokes about their necks.

'Koosh, koosh, koosh. Come on Frith. Move, you dumb ox,' coaxed a lad, placing the heavy wooden yoke over the animal's neck. The work continued while the women repacked the wagons and rounded up the children.

Snapping their whips and whistling stringent notes, the outriders moved the wagons into a column as the leader shouted the roll-call.

'Van Heerden?'

'Ya,' a voice came from the first wagon. A lad in the front of the span of oxen pulled the reins. The beasts behind him took the strain. Wooden wheels creaked as the wagon shifted.

'Master Jones?'

'Aye.'

The second wagon followed.

'Sir Auston?' Giggles came from the young girls sitting in the nearest wagon. Sir Auston, indeed. How singular? Miss Auston hearing the giggles tucked her skirt well under her knees, sat primly and ignored the laughter. Her father answered.

'Present, sir.'

The leader continued the roll-call.

4

'Dimenco?'

'*Si.*'

'MacPhearson?'

The wagon remained stationary.

'MacPhearson!' came the authoritative voice. 'Where's your voor-loper?'

Behind a bush a small boy hastily pulled up his ragged pants.

'I'm coming. I'm coming,' he shouted and rushed to the front of his team. 'Koosh, koosh,' urged the boy. The strange sound of the words soothed the oxen and they responded. The wagon rolled forward.

'Vosoki, Kessler, Brown, O'Rielly, are you ready?'

As soon as the roll-call was completed, the march began. Each wagon threw long shadows over the veld as the sun tipped the rim of the horizon.

A baritone started singing a hymn of praise and thanks for their daily food, a peaceful night, the health of their members. Everyone gave thanks for the marvel they had seen, a perfect rainbow across a waterfall.

All day long a dust trail, as if attached to the last wagon, followed the trek and mingled with the fragrance of the blossoming acacia. Farming equipment and tools rattled and dishes and utensils clattered against the sides of the wagons. Tables, chairs, iron bedsteads shifted to the swaying of the carts. Ornate clocks, precious platters and family heirlooms clinked together in the tin trunks as the carts teetered over the stony tracks. Voices called to one another. Children laughed. Babies fretted.

Older and stronger boys helped by pushing the wagons up the inclines. The men, their hands calloused and fingernails broken, gripped the spokes and forced the wagon wheels to turn. On the descent the men strained their leg muscles to take the weight of the carts against their backs. Teenage girls walked beside the wagons carrying blackened pots and every so often they stooped over the wheels of the carts to grease the axles with fat rendered from wild game. The carts moved forward, inch by cart-creaking inch.

5

Three outriders, flailing their horses, worked up and down the column, helping where necessary. They retrieved wandering children and shot marauding leopards and wild dogs scavenging for morsels of food. Pausing occasionally to drink boiled water from a canvas bag, the riders cajoled the teams throughout the day.

From the bank of the crocodile-infested river an outrider splashed into the water before the wagons attempted to cross. Yelling and beating the water, he rode to the opposite bank. Once there, he round his horse and returned. The lurking crocodiles, with mean little eyes, smiling jaws and horned-tails, slid away. More often a hippopotamus appeared to open its rubbery mouth, yawn, then sink below the surface.

'Green and greasy where the fever trees grow.' That's how Rudyard Kipling described the Limpopo River. After months of weary travel, the adventurers approached the river banks. They found an arid expanse of yielding sand. Mirages and heat waves shimmered over swelling dunes and clusters of spiked bronzed rushes. Weeping willows slumped over the banks. Their brittle fronds, lamenting for moisture, hung over the blistering sand.

'Is there no other place where we can cross?' asked the leader.

'Fifty miles to the east the river bed narrows but the banks are steep and dangerous,' answered the guide.

'Then we must unpack our belongings and ford the river here.'

'We can't pull the wagons through the sand.' Jones spoke for the travellers.

'We'll dismantle them and haul each section across.'

The project began. Men and women strapped sections of the wagons on their backs. They resembled huge alien beetles as they zigged-zagged over the squeaky sand. Day after day the back-breaking struggle continued. Three weeks later, the crossing was completed, the travellers reassembled the wagons and went on their way.

They reached the range of amethyst mountains that blocked their passage to the west. Tirelessly, the guides on

6

horseback searched and found the old route around and over the mountains.

'Warriors are hiding in the hills,' the scout reported to the leader. 'We are entering a narrow strip of grassland. On each side of us, to the north and south there are warring tribes. Tomorrow we will enter that passage. You had better caution the column.'

'Friends,' said the leader to the group as they sat around the fire. 'Tomorrow we begin our trek through a land peopled by warriors. Our scouts have seen them watching us from the granite outcrops. Sometimes the natives are aggressive and will attack travellers, we can never be certain. We have no other choice but to take the chance and go forward. The hostile people may be jittery and nervous of our presence.'

'Why won't they attack us?' asked MacPhearson.

'It is difficult to say. Maybe they are preparing, after the heavy rains, for their seasonal raid on their enemies to the south. We might be safe as long as we keep moving and not let them see our weapons or anything they might fancy.'

'We will have to take the chance and travel as fast as possible,' said Kessler.

'I came this way with the pioneer column five years ago. The natives were peaceful then and let us through,' said the leader.

MacPhearson, thinking aloud said, 'I wonder why this . . . this corridor seems to be no-man's land.'

'Maybe there is an agreement between the tribes not to occupy this stretch of land,' said the leader. 'Or maybe it's infested with the malaria mosquito.'

'Let's hope there is no tsetse fly here. They carry the parasite that causes sleeping sickness,' said van Heerden, as he surveyed the teams of oxen.

'The children – what about the children, they will be bitten,' wailed a mother.

'They can be kept covered. It's the oxen we can't afford to lose before we have reached our destination.'

'But our children . . .'

'Our supplies and tools must be hidden,' the leader interrupted. 'The women will hide in the wagons and the children stay quiet. Don't outspan the oxen at night for we must be well on our way before daylight. If there is enough moonlight we'll keep moving throughout the night.'

Quietly as possible and steadily the column crept through the narrow passage. Children and women crammed in the wagons clutching anything that might rattle. All eyes were on the lookout for any hidden faces or sudden movement. At night they formed tighter laagers and ate hastily cooked meals. While the travellers slept, the night guards watched and waited. At the slightest noise they either twisted around or cowered in fright. Shadows appeared in scary shapes.

'What's that?' the watcher whispered. Sweaty fingers tightened around the rifle. Images of spears about to pierce the body or black hands squeezing the throat were bright and vivid in the mind's eye. Cold and weary, the explorers huddled against the wagon wheels. The guards desperately craved sleep.

The shadows darkened.

'There! There, it's coming!' a terrified boy flinched.

'Hold still, it's the clouds. They are coming in from the west,' a calming voice replied.

Throughout the day, as their wagons creaked along the valley floor the travellers anticipated hordes of warriors on the attack. High on the granite hills, unseen warriors held assegais, deadly and slender as javelins. Stealthily, they slipped among the boulders watching the small train of wagons below.

In the moonlight a lad held out a bucket of water. 'Here Frith, drink.' The animal lowered its head. There was no relief from the weight of the heavy yoke upon its neck.

Outriders worked harder, circling the convoy repeatedly. To the south of them a tribe of small agile men like a pack of hyenas trailed the column, waiting for easy pickings – a straggling wagon, a lost child.

With the open lands giving way to shrubs and thorn trees, the tension of the journey eased. The settlers had overcome their ordeal. Once again the children laughed and the people sang.

After two years of dragging their goods and shackles, the travellers reached the small settlement of Ashvale. Their wanderings had ended.

As the years passed, the descendants of the pioneers and settlers clustered their houses around the base of Pioneer Hill. They lived unpretentious lives and valued their isolation. Jealously, they guarded their privilege to be as they were. Master Jones and the prim Miss Auston joined names and souls in holy wedlock. Like their fellow travellers, they farmed their land, planted trees and gardens and built their home.

The population grew rapidly when the railhead reached the colony. Immigrants flocked into the country. Each having personal reasons to leave the land of their birth. They travelled by rail or over the dusty highway from the south. Settlers came seeking refuge from religious persecution. Refugees from the rape of the Boer War and misplaced persons from the First World War increased the population. Entrepreneurs arrived to search for the promised riches, compelling their families to endure the hardships of an untamed land.

Chapter 2

Two small hands, grimy and lacerated from scavenging in rubbish bins, appeared under the rotting wooden crate. The box rose a fraction, disturbing tiny fruit flies and the stench from a mound of decaying produce that lay nearby. Once again the box lifted, high enough for a yellow-skinned urchin to poke his head from his temporary sleeping quarters. He twitched his nostrils as the nauseating stench reached his nose and he blinked away the onslaught of minute flies. Malnutrition, not the genes in his blood, caused the ginger colour in his fuzzy hair. A genealogist would have found it difficult to trace this urchin's roots. His ancestors may have been of Indian origin or of British descent. Perhaps they had travelled from distant lands. Huguenot, Chinese labourers, Malays, Dutch, French and Germans had drifted to the shores of Africa during the past centuries.

His mother was indigenous. Maybe her bloodline was from the Kulu, Xhosi or a clan from the remote interior? Twelve years ago, when gold miners spent freely, she had charged a shilling for her favours, but times had forced the price down to a sixpence. The year 1930, the time of the great depression, was difficult for the entrepreneur. The urchin never considered the price of his conception. From an early age he roamed in the alleys of Johannesburg scavenging for his daily bread.

Another wave of rankness from the decaying heap of vegetables wafted across his face and made him twitch and blink once more. For so long he had endured the stench, the spasmodic tic had become an unconscious habit when each new thought entered his head. Tonight in the damp dreary evening the smell was overpowering. Sickened by the stench, he scrambled to his feet and, keeping close to the wall, made his way to the open market. Sounds of shunting locomotives clattering came from afar. Occasionally a stray animal slunk across the street and disappeared through a gap in the wall. Southern winds, bitterly cold winds, gnawed at the awnings of the makeshift stalls and forced the marketeers to huddle under their cloaks and shawls. Crumpled newspapers carried by the wind, scraped against the cracked and stained brick walls, as ghostly satanic forms, created by the evening mist moved over the sidewalks. Other shapes in human forms, hurried to the warmth and comfort in their homes.

On this cold evening the urchin felt very hungry. He crept close to a stall. Eyes above a dark muffler glared at him. He scuttled past. At the next stall the boy saw two succulent pears glowing in the dull light. They sat like twins on the edge of the wooden counter. He bent low, lower than the stall and crept nearer. Slowly he raised his hand to grab the luscious fruit.

Whack! The leather strap stung his hand. With a sharp cry he fell against the stand. Down came the produce. An apple rolled past him into the gutter. Snatching it, the urchin darted down the street and disappeared into the misty night. Tightly holding the booty against his chest, he ran on until he saw two rubbish bins against the wall. He crouched behind them and, hidden and protected from the thin wind, bit into the fruit. Spittle dripped as he greedily gobbled the fruit. He reached the core and was about to stuff it, pips and all into his mouth when heavy footsteps approached. He held still, listening.

Cautiously, he raised his head and saw a small procession coming down the street. A stout woman, breathing strenuously, came first. She carried a bulging leather purse in one gloved hand and a tote bag in the other. A shapeless felt hat covered her brow. Her winter coat added bulk to her already heavy frame. Hattie, her five-year-old daughter, followed at

12

a distance. The hem of her coat flapped around her ankles and the sleeves reached below her hands.

'Hurry up Hattie,' the mother commanded.

Hattie took a longer stride and almost tripped over her ill-fitting coat. She stopped and looked over her shoulder. The urchin saw her eyes, unusual smoky lilac eyes that opened wide as she twisted around and said, 'Mama! They're not coming.'

The mother stopped, impatiently tapped her small foot in a worn leather shoe and waited for an old man. He staggered up with a black trunk wobbling on his shoulder. Tattered clothing hung loosely over his thin frame. Skeletal fingers, blue with cold, gripped the metal handle on the trunk. His frozen breath came from an unseen mouth hidden under a sloughed hat.

'Come along or we'll be late,' the mother ordered.

The tin trunk tilted precariously as the old man stopped in front of the stout woman.

'Agh missus,' said he allowing the trunk to fall to the ground. 'I can't carry this trunk, it's too heavy.' With those words he walked away.

'Seth, can you lift it?' asked the woman.

'No Ma,' answered the twelve-year-old boy who tagged behind the old man. 'It's too big.'

'Ask him to help. He looks like a waif but I bet he's strong,' said Hattie pointing to the urchin.

The urchin stepped forward wiping the back of his hand across his mouth.

'How much?'

The mother set the tote bag down, opened her bag and held out four pennies. To the urchin, the coins shining in the street lamp looked like nuggets of gold. Four pennies were wealth indeed for a homeless waif, enough to buy two meat pies. Meat pies filled with dark rich juices.

Taking the old man's place, he lifted the trunk on to his shoulder and asked. 'To the trains?'

Answering his question with a nod, the woman and the children continued walking to the railway station. They

13

passed through the towering marble pillars to reach the concourse.

'Seth, mind Hattie while I get the tickets. You,' the mother said pointing to the urchin, 'wait with the luggage.'

Hattie wriggled her skinny buttocks on the bench and mumbled from the folds of her coat. 'I hate this thing, it's too big for me, and it is a horrid colour. It's greasy green like the creepies that live in puddles of water.'

Hattie looked up at the domed rotunda. In the distance whistles shrieked, engines puffed and hot steam rose from under wooden coaches.

'This big place with the round roof way up there frightens me. I wish I was at home again,' she said.

'You can't go back because Ma sold everything. She even sold the old faded lino in the passage. Remember the square patterns on it.'

Hattie chose not to hear Seth. She wanted to be back in the little brick house that she had known all her life.

'I wonder if the old lady next door is watering her flowers. I love those big flowers with bright colours. They grow big as bread-and-butter plates. I know 'cos I could see them through the gap in the tin fence.'

Hattie fell silent. After a little while in a soft voice she asked, 'Where're we going, Seth?'

'Far away. Way out into the bush, to another place. Pioneers found this strange country years ago.'

Seth spoke the truth. They were on their way like so many other immigrants to make a new home in the north.

'What's a pioneer?'

'A man who goes looking for new lands. Don't ask such silly questions.' Seth frowned at his sister.

'Why didn't Daddy go back to work in the mine?' asked Hattie.

'Because he was coughing too much. Remember all the blood on his handkerchief. Now he has gone to look for gold. I wonder if he got there. The old truck might have fallen to bits. He said the road was all dusty and bumpy. That's why we are going by train.'

14

Hattie sighed. 'When'll we get there, Seth?'

The boy ran his hand through his red hair and swung his legs. He did not know the answer. Hattie always asked too many questions. 'About five days,' he said finally.

'That's far away. Are there lions and tigers and animals like that?'

'No tigers in Africa silly, only enormous leopards and lions live there. Also long and fat snakes live in the dry grass. They slither up trees and twist around the branches. They crawl into your bed at night.'

'Those creatures won't frighten me,' said Hattie.

'What about cannibals? They'll scare you, 'cos they eat people and they dance like this.'

Seth jumped off the bench. He pulled up the legs of his pants exposing his knobbly knees. On bent skinny legs and waggling his backside, he tried to do a tribal war dance. The urchin blinked and twitched his lips as he watched the girl with strange-coloured eyes laughing at her brother's antics.

'You'll always make me laugh. You're too funny to frighten me, Seth.' Looking up at the urchin, Hattie asked, 'What's your name?'

'Pete,' he answered.

'Pete who? Haven't you got another name?'

The lad shrugged.

'Mines Henrietta Carver, but everyone calls me Hattie. I don't know where we are going. Somewhere far away . . . there's my mother coming back with the tickets.'

'Come now. No dawdling,' said Mrs Carver as she gathered her small family and hustled them down the platform.

'Here, this is our coach,' she said while checking the numbers on the coach against the ticket in her hand. 'I'll get in and find our compartment. Seth, help the boy and hand me the cases through the window.'

'Lift the trunks onto your shoulder Pete, then I'll push,' said Seth. He stretched up and eased the luggage through the window. Hattie watched the two youths struggling with the luggage and thought how much she hated the tin trunk. Its shape and blackness frightened and depressed her. Hattie

15

was sure the trunk was filled with dark and frightening secrets.

When all the cases were stowed into the compartment and the family settled in, Mrs Carver handed Pete his earnings. 'Here is your money: four pennies.'

With his ginger hair fuzzed out like a bottle-brush, the boy skipped off down the platform. The four pennies jangled in the pocket of his tattered shorts – carrying goods was a profitable business. Hattie called from the compartment window but he was too far away to hear. 'Bye Pete. We won't meet again, for I'm going far away.'

Far down the line the guard leaned out of his caboose, waved a flag and blew a shrill blast on his whistle. Up ahead the engine driver acknowledged the signals and pulled his head back into the cab. The locomotive belched a plume of coal dust. Metal ground against metal, the wheels began to turn. Coaches rattled as the couplings took up the slack and slowly the train slithered out of the station. Like a serpent casting off its moulted skin, the coaches wriggled forward. The marketplace, the urchin Pete, and the street lamps faded into the night.

The train chugged over dry veld and past jagged hills. Stunted thorn trees grew in the poor soil. Small scavengers slunk under the dry brush that fringed the Kalahari Desert. A roan antelope stood, silhouetted against a backdrop of blue sky. Sunlight rippled from its dark-brown hide, antlers curving gracefully above its noble head.

'Look Seth, a unicorn,' said Hattie clapping her hands.

'Don't be silly, it's an antelope. It has two antlers,' her brother answered.

At bedtime, Hattie lay on the top bunk watching her mother. She could see and feel her mother's despair as the stout woman stood gazing into the black night. Finally, Hattie heard a sigh and the window shut. In the reflection of the pane Hattie watched her mother sponge her arms and sagging bosom in the small basin. What would happen to them in this wild and untamed land?

For three cool nights and four hot days the monotonous

journey continued, to where the elephant and lion, warthog, lizards and reptiles live. To the mighty rivers where the crocodiles laze in tepid waters. Where the fish-eagle calls it haunting cry. The family continued their journey to the land where the msasa trees grow.

Three years later Seth, now a lad of fourteen, emerged from the long grass. Without hesitation he leaped off the high bank, his red hair and old jacket billowing behind him. Landing on all fours in the sand, he stood up and brushed his hands on his shirt. He stepped with his bare feet, disregarding the hot pebbles, into the river bed.

Sand dunes and rounded stones, heavy with mica, pyrite and flecked with gold, made an irregular bed for the river. A river carved aeons ago. Ever flowing east, it often curved back on itself as if to brood like a mourner wending its way through narrow streets. Slowly it flowed, turgid and dark between banks of dark red earth. At times it skirted mountains then narrowed through gorges. It bubbled over shallow rapids and meandered sedately through the reeds. Over the years the current eroded the banks and altered its course.

Some summers the river god became a fickle god and just for spite it would shrink the river to a paltry trickle. Then during the next season it might be generous and allow the wayside ponds to overflow. These pools became stagnant during the winter dry season.

This past summer the river god had been indulgent for the rains were good. The pools throughout the winter and spring remained full. Now just before the seasonal rains, it regretted that past generosity. The river god darkened the northern clouds with water. They became so heavy that they burst. The river swelled to generate a monstrous flood that swept away everything in its path. This river god was searching for a scapegoat upon which to vent its wrath.

On this sunny morning, Hattie stood in a pool and watched Seth in the distance. He picked up a rock, gave it a rub on his khaki pants and peered at it. Finally, he spat on it, shone and inspected it again then tossed it away. Hattie

17

knew he was looking for gold. She hoped he would find a large nugget so her father could sell it and buy real meat and potatoes and jelly. She had grown tired of their staple diet, venison, ground corn, and endless cups of hot tea.

Hattie watched her brother continue his search as the heat waves lingered above the sand dunes and glittering rocks in the river bed. A mirage danced over the distant savanna. Long dry grass swayed to the rhythm of the cicada's high-pitched melody. Winter had passed. In the springtime, the woodlands filled with the colourful leaves of the msasa trees: orange, russet, silver, greens and gold. The warmth of spring encouraged the sap to rise from deep within the African earth.

Hattie cupped her hands against her mouth to shout across the river.

'Seth, you make me laugh the way you stalk on skinny legs like the crested crane. It has a funny mop of feathers on its head. Dad's old coat sticking out behind you, looks like folded wings. Why are you wearing that coat when it's so hot?'

'So I can carry my samples of gold,' Seth yelled.

'But there's no gold in the river,' Hattie yelled back.

'Other prospectors have been here, so there must be gold.'

Exploring the countryside Hattie and Seth had found prospectors' diggings and crumbling foundations, a testimonial to someone's hopes and dreams. Their father shared the same delusions. Since the tedious train journey three years ago, the family had wandered from place to place searching for gold.

In a dilapidated truck they carted their few belongings from one site to another. Seth and Hattie huddled on the back, the mining equipment rattling beside them. Over old tracks and sometimes over the grasslands they went, deeper and deeper into the interior, farther and farther from civilisation.

Hattie remembered the day her father found a few ounces of gold.

'We must buy the children new shoes,' her mother said.

18

But Hattie's father said they must wait because they needed another vehicle. A prospector was leaving the country and had an old Ford to sell. Hattie could never understand why Seth agreed with his father. The vehicle became the centre of the boy's existence.

'Look at the headlights, they're magnificent. Listen to the engine,' he went on, 'purrs like a cat.'

'Rubbish, it's old and rusty,' said Hattie, 'I'd rather have new shoes.' Such were her hopes and dreams.

Hattie watched Seth fill his pockets with stones until he shouted from across the river. 'Other miners found gold here.'

'Where are they now, if there is gold here?' she answered. Her voice echoed down the river bed.

Seth blushed, and felt uncomfortable with Hattie's reasoning. To get even he shouted back. 'Hattie, come out of that pool! Ma told me to mind you. She said you must not play in the pools. There's bilharzia in there. Where are your sandals?'

'I've tied them onto my belt.'

'Come out of the water. You know you must not play in the still water.'

'The sand's too hot. There are only tadpoles and funny black worms and insects in here. Can't see any bilharzia.'

'Silly, of course you can't see bilharzia. They're tiny worms and they get into your tummy.'

'How can bilharzia get into my tummy? I'm not sitting in the water.'

Girls! They ask such silly questions, Seth thought. 'Through the scratches on your legs. Never know when it will eat at your insides.'

Seth went back to his prospecting for gold. Eight-year-old females never listen. Hattie, unafraid of insects, happily picked them up to scrutinise them. One day a scorpion or something will bite her and that will be the end. Seth, forgetting about his sister, found a likely looking specimen of gold. He put it in his pocket.

Water lilies grew in the pool. Hattie pulled one and it came away with minute black snails sticking to the long brown stems. Bending and twisting the tentacles, she tried to free them from the flower. The stems were too tough and leathery so she threw the plant into the stagnant water and washed the scum from her hands.

Above the cicada's high-pitched chirping, Hattie heard the sound of a wheelbarrow and the rattling of two large cans. Oparee, a native in his early twenties, came to the river to fill the cans with water. Originally they held paraffin, until someone had fashioned them into crude pails with a jagged edge around the rims. Scrambling down the bank and splashing through the widening stream Oparee came to Hattie's pool. He couldn't understand the white folk. They washed in hot water every night. Why didn't they bathe in the river?

As he picked up the second can he pointed to the weaver's nest and said. 'When river god happy the birds know. They put their nest high, very high. No good rains when the weavers build in the low branches of the mutepe. River god very, very angry.'

Oparee smiled his perpetual smile. His beautiful white teeth brightened his round ebony face. Hattie had seen him polishing his teeth with a splayed twig from the mutepe tree.

'You know a lot about the birds and animals.'

'Yes, my grandfather taught me many years ago.'

'You lived here a long time?'

'No. Not long, only two seasons. When the soil becomes poor my family will go to another place. Sometimes we join other tribes. When the clan becomes too big we divide again and seek new pastures or hunting grounds.'

Behind them the sound of the stream grew louder. Neither Oparee nor Hattie noticed the change in the river. They went on talking while Hattie splashed about in the pool. 'Will you go away with your family?'

'No, when I leave here I'll go to the city to learn to drive a bus. My brother went to the city in one.'

'I've never been to the city,' sighed Hattie. 'You better get the water to Mama, she will be getting mad.'

20

Oparee filled the second can and splashed through the current, back to his barrow.

'Tell Seth, he is on the other side of the river, to teach you to drive that silly old car,' Hattie called to Oparee as she waded deeper in the pool. She stopped, listened. Something had changed. The river, it flowed faster and deeper.

Seth had walked farther up the river bed.

'Look at the river Seth! Seth! Look! The river – it's rising,' she yelled.

Seth looked up. His body stiffened as he scanned the river ahead. Mesmerised, he stood for twenty seconds then turned and ran, throwing the rocks from his pockets. Hattie giggled as she watched him run back to the bank and plastered himself against the red earth. His long arms snatched for a hold on the grass above his head as his bare feet gouged the bank. At last he found a foothold and pulled himself up to safety. He vanished through the yellow grass.

The river god's cloud had burst, sending the water raging into a roaring torrent. Hattie had to cross the water for her home stood on the other side. Wading out of the pool, she began to run over the dunes. Soft burning sand gave way under her footsteps, hampering her progress. At last she came to the brink of the water and hesitated, afraid of the fast-flowing current. There was no choice but to try to cross.

She plunged into the stream and slipped on the muddy river bed. Down she went, tumbling over and over. The current threw her against the bank as she surfaced, gasping for air. She snatched at a clump of earth but it came away in her hands. Faster and faster the current pulled her down the river. In desperation she grasped at an overhanging branch of the mutepe and hoisted herself half out of the water.

For a moment she clung to the branch, as the surging water deafened all other sounds. She looked back and saw a tumbling mass of uprooted trees, islands of weeds and churning debris surging towards her. Above the turmoil rose a hideous monster with repulsive antlers, sharp as rapiers.

21

Yellow foam washed over its parted lips and eyes, opened in death. The distended body came directly at her.

Using all her strength, Hattie pulled at the branch, reached the side of the bank and dragged herself up.

'Seth! Seth.' Her voice was pitifully weak. She called again. 'Where are you Seth? Help me. Please Seth.' Where was her minder, her mentor, her only companion? No one heard her cries.

The image of the distended beast spurred her on. Trying to suppress the frightening vision, she covered her face with her bent arm and ran. Sharp rocks and spiked grass ripped her bare feet until she became aware of her sandals hanging from her belt. Sitting on a large boulder she wiped the soil from her feet and slipped on her sandals. Lost and alone the little girl glanced around, the landscape was unfamiliar. Which way should she go?

Hattie left the rock and wandered aimlessly until she came to a rough road overgrown by grass and weeds. She followed the road until it dwindled into a single path. On she walked until the path ended close to a msasa tree, its spreading branches offering shade and peace. Hattie sat to rest.

A swishing of branches sounded in the far-off trees. The rustling came nearer and nearer accompanied by shrieking and chattering. Hattie remained still, petrified. Thump. Thump. A heavy body landed in a tree close by. Hattie lifted her head. Two black marble eyes in a black furry face stared down at her. It was the leader of a troop of vervet monkeys. He glared sternly at her for a moment, and then decided she was harmless. With a quick leap to a higher branch, the monkey gave a piercing yell.

In twos and threes the families arrived. Infants with enchantingly ugly faces clung to their mother's backs. Aunts, uncles, brothers and sisters came chattering by. The animals broke twigs and snapped the dry pods of the mufufu tree. They nibbled at some of the pods and dropped the rest. Ceaselessly jabbering, they swung from tree to tree. In the wake of the monkeys came the browsers. Duiker with their short twisted horns and impala on dainty hooves fed on the dropped leaves. Bushbuck who preferred the pods came next. Ox-eyed birds settled on the animals to clean parasites from their hides. White egrets fed on insects that the browsing animals disturbed as they nibbled the grass. Slowly the parade of woodland creatures moved along, following the monkeys' trail.

Hattie rested her head on her arms and fell asleep. A small herd of elephant came lumbering through the grass. In the centre of the herd a baby bull elephant trotted, protected by four young females and a matriarch. The smaller creatures in the woodland evaded the elephant's soft tread and bulky presence. The matriarch swayed her trunk over the ground before placing her massive foot by the sleeping child. Then with a swish of her large ears and lurch of the massive body, the grey tusker quietly turned and led her family away. From the branch of the msasa tree a repulsive spider dropped in the first silken thread of her web above the sleeping child.

Suddenly a hollow sound, wood thumping against wood in a steady rhythm, echoed through the woodlands.

Chapter 3

The unearthly clamour ricocheted from tree to tree muffling the normal sound of the forest, the chirping of birds, the scuttling of rodents through the long grass and the bark of the hyena.

A tall woman, Leena was causing the unusual noise. She stood above a wooden mortar made from the trunk of a hollowed tree and crushed corn kernels with a heavy club. As she crushed the corn into a fine flour the sound of wood against wood resounded through the trees. Sweat silvered her ebony skin as her strong arms raised and lowered the pole. A pale blue cloth, the colour bleached by years of laundering, hung gracefully from her waist.

A grey lourie in the tree opened its sharp beak and shrieked an alarming cry: 'Go-way . . . go-way-way.' Then raising its crest and after preening a feather, the bird flew into the next tree. A red squirrel heeded the bird's warning and scurried into the hollow of a log. The flock of guinea fowl cackled and scattered in different directions. In their frenzy they ran past the safety of the brush.

Leena crushed the corn for a few more minutes then knelt to rekindle her fire by blowing gently on glowing coals. Small flames soon began to lick the dried twigs. Years ago Leena had built her hearth of three flat stones. The open hearth glowing with warm amber coals and wisps of smoke was home to her son, Jourbor. In his mother's presence and close to the hearth he felt secure.

Leena reached for her broom of tied brush and began to

sweep her yard when a shadow darkened the mellow light on the path. She cringed. What kind of animal watched her? As a figure emerged from the trees she backed into the doorway of a thatched hut.

'Greetings,' a resonant voice called.

Leena stepped from her shelter as a dignified stranger came down the path. He raised his left hand, palm facing her as a sign of friendship. Leena dropped her broom and went to meet him.

'Please stay for as long as you wish,' she gave her traditional greeting.

They touched hands. Leena bobbed a curtsy for a person should respect long whiskers and tight greying curls. Miles of wandering had hardened the soles of his bare feet and cracked his heels. A leopard's skin covered his back, its paws reached to his thighs. From his belt hung an old leather pouch and several large dead rodents.

Leena eyed the fat rodents. Meat and salt had been hard to come by recently.

'Who are you? Where do you live?' she asked.

'My name is M'kama. I am a hunter, a storyteller, and a poet,' he answered and waved a hand to encompass the world about him. 'I live close by.'

She acknowledged his reply by a modest lift of one shoulder as if sceptical of his credentials and 'close by' could be many miles away.

'When did you leave your house?'

'When the green speckled dove awoke and began to call and the moonbeams faded in the east.' He pointed dramatically at the horizon.

'Oh.' Leena answered, unaffected by the stranger's poetic licence and sense of the dramatic. She eyed the rodents again, for she lived in a world of reality.

For a long while they stood appraising each other. She decided that he came from a peaceful tribe across the mountains. He recognised the clan markings over her temples. Her forefathers were once an influential tribe who occupied much

26

land in the west. Over the years the tribe had divided into groups that alienated themselves.

M'kama noted the tidy yard and a white goat tethered to a shrub. Two speckled hens scratched in the brown earth. There were five neatly thatched huts surrounding the hearth. An extended family lived in the small settlement and most likely the menfolk were following the trails of the game.

'Is the hunting good?' Leena asked.

M'kama compressed his lips and shook the spear. 'No, the animals have roamed to the north. The rains have come to pass. Now the black earth is mint green with new grass. Herds of beasts graze. The duiker will come. Safe in numbers, bigger game gathers in the open. The warthog bends his knees in prayer. Giraffe will reach to the topmost branch of the muunga to nibble the leaves. Do you know what the elephant does? He . . .'

'Yes, he rubs against the tree to rid his hide of ticks. Like this,' Leena answered and waggled her buttocks. 'If the trees are old they'll fall over.'

'Oh. Oh,' said M'kama taken by surprise at Leena's knowledge of the elephant. He smiled at the handsome woman. His eyes matched the brown berries on the shrubs nearby.

'My son Jourbor is at the river, I must call him.' Leena walked past the huts and called. 'Jourbor . . . aiee . . . aiee.' The sharp notes in the melody of her voice echoed through the woodlands.

'Go-way . . . go-way-way,' the lourie screeched again and small animals darted for cover.

M'kama and Leena moved into the shade of the mimosa tree where the bees hummed busily around the fragrant yellow puffed blossoms. Close by, the tethered goat nibbled on the shrub. Leena sat on the ground with her legs extended and M'kama made himself comfortable on a rock above her. Tradition demanded that one's betters always sat above oneself.

A small boy six years of age appeared. He was naked save for a string of red and black beans around his protruding stomach. The beans were lucky because the gods opened the

27

hardy pods. On hot days at the end of summer when the air is dry the pods burst open with a resounding crack. Only tree gods could do that.

Leena motioned to the boy. 'Come sit, Jourbor.'

He was her only child, a strange lad never wanting to hunt or play rough games like other boys. He'd rather remain by the hearth carving wood or modelling the red clay. Maybe his difficult birth made him so different.

'Giving birth is easier if you widen your birth canal with your clenched fist,' the midwife advised the pregnant Leena. Each day Leena followed the advice but it didn't help at the time of birth. The midwife clicked her tongue as Leena screamed with excruciating labour pains. No herbs or magic spells eased her distress. Eight hours later the baby arrived, buttocks first and his arms and legs entangled around his body.

Jourbor approached his mother and the visitor. He held his head away from the stranger. Children do not look at their elders until spoken to. Leena waited until Jourbor sat beside her.

'Where are you going, famous hunter?' she asked.

'To see the white gods; they live nearby. The witch doctor told me they eat sand that is white and sweet.'

Jourbor cuddled close to his mother. Scepticism came to Leena's deep brown eyes. Bah! The only sweetness she had tasted came from the hives of the wild bees. *White* gods! No. She knew about all the gods, the tree god and the mountain god, but she had never heard of white gods.

'What do you mean, white?'

M'kama pointed to the goat's rump. 'Like that.'

She pulled back aghast, then grasped the idea. These gods have white hair over their bodies.

'Oh,' she replied, the notion was beyond her imagination. 'From where do these gods come?'

'Out of the big, very big water. That is why they are white.'

The woman shrugged her shoulder again, her facial expression giving nothing away, but still eyeing the rodents.

'These gods, they make marks on stuff like . . .' he searched for a likeness, 'like leaves. They draw lines and make marks with sticks. Other gods understand the marks.'

M'kama hoped this item of interest would stop Leena's interrogation. She reminded him of his second wife, the fat one with two children. The wife who was always talking and wanting his belongings. She demanded his choicest pelts for her son and the claws of his leopard for her daughter. His second wife asked questions, too many questions he found difficult to answer.

Leena dismissed the idea of marks and leaves and said. 'What is this big, very big water?'

M'kama stood up, leaned on his spear, his buttocks protruding. He rubbed his head and scratched his nose. After a deep thought he answered.

'You have felt the earth breath deeply before a storm?'

Leena nodded.

'And you have seen the grassland that never ends?'

'Yes, it begins just over the hill.' She faced the west and pointed.

'You have heard the earth blow out her breath and then the grass bends over this way and that way. This way and that way.' M'kama swayed his body from right to left. 'All the way out of sight the grass shifts but never moves. Well, the big, very big water moves like the grass and at night the sun sinks into it.' He returned to the rock and sat with hands folded across his chest, his head held high.

'Oh,' replied Leena.

Both friends were silent, reflecting.

'How do you know all this?' asked Leena.

'Drums. The drums told us.'

This made sense. Leena's lively brown eyes showed no surprise. She nodded her head. Those drummers never lie. Often she had heard the throbs rolling over the hilltops and through the valleys. She taught Jourbor to interpret the rhythms. They told of strange or exciting events. They relayed the route of the migration of antelope herds and the expectations of floods. Drummers sent news of a chief's son's marriage. There were times when the drummers predicted

29

the death of a river god or a tree god. Leena waited for M'kama to continue.

'Yes. The drums said the white gods are insignificant gods,' he continued eventually. 'I am told they're silly and their children have thin legs and arms. The fathers dig holes in the ground looking for yellow stones and mothers wear head-dresses, soft as thistledown and pretty like the seventh colour of the rainbow. Yes, the white gods have strange ways. One day they will rule over us.'

'What is the difference? Dictators and chiefs from many tribes have dominated us in the past. They rule the land for a few seasons then fade away. It makes no difference. The sun still rises and the rains come. Since our ancestors were children, they heard the emerald-spotted dove's call. So do we. It's the pulse of earth that dictates our lives.'

With that remark Leena left her place and fetched an earthenware pot filled with water from her hut. Rekindling the fire, she put the pot of water on to boil and added the ground corn. M'kama undid the rodents from his belt and gave them to her. With a sharp stone she scraped the hair from the animals and quickly removed the entrails with one practised movement. From the folds of her skirt she brought out a handful of herbs. These she sprinkled over the rodents and placed them on the hot coals. As the water heated, Leena added her ground corn and gently stirred until it cooked into porridge.

Leena looked at the pouch tied to her visitor's belt of woven reeds and hinted: 'Salt would be good?'

M'kama unfastened his pouch from his belt and untied the cord. The pouch contained a variety of roots.

'This one,' he explained to Leena, 'will cure headaches. This is to clear the stomach from parasites that breed in the river.'

'The parasites live in the snails that breed in the pools. I use a green herb to cure the disease that the parasites carry.'

M'kama pulled down his mouth, and thought: This woman knows a lot.

'Here,' he said and broke off a small piece of coarse salt

30

from a larger tablet. The colourless crystals on their long journey from the Sahara had changed hands many times. Salt miners used this condiment to barter for wives or ivory, pelts or potent mixtures. Here salt was more precious than gold.

M'kama condescended to speak to the child. 'Greetings my son. What have you in your hand?'

The boy held out a clay tablet.

'What have you drawn on it?'

'This is me,' Jourbor pointed to a figure kneeling. 'This bowl which I hold is filled with my wishes. I'm giving it to the eagle, see there, to take to the Mighty One.'

'What are your wishes?'

'To be brave like my father and one day maybe do kind deeds.'

'I'm sure they will come true,' laughed M'kama.

Leena clicked her tongue. 'He is always dreaming or playing with clay or carving wood. Please come to the fire and share our meal.'

The three diners dipped their hands into the pot. Each took a small portion of corn porridge and rolled it into a ball, before popping into their mouths. The porridge and the grilled rodents made a substantial meal. After dinner, Leena handed a gourd of goats' milk to her guest. He took a long drink and gave the gourd back to her.

'How many wives and children have you?' Leena asked politely.

He held up three fingers. 'My first wife is old now. I called the second one "Shoko" because she chatters like the big grey monkey. She gave me two children. My son is very tall and handsome. The girl,' M'kama pouted his lips sadly, 'her one eye looks to the east the other to the north. She'll never find a husband.'

'And my boy here, he was born in a strange way. The gods were unfair to us.'

Leena and M'kama covered their heads with their hands and softly clicked their tongues, commiserating over their misfortunes. A tear rolled down Jourbor's soft cheek. Above

31

them a locust took flight, its translucent wings hovering on the hot air. From nowhere a black bird, the drongo, swept down, and snatched the insect and impaled it on a thorn of the mimosa tree.

Drying her eyes with the palm of her hand, Leena turned her attention to her visitor. 'Have you any other children?' she asked.

'Eight. My youngest wife gave me a daughter. She will give me fine sons.'

With a sharp click of her tongue she answered. 'Yaa.'

'Will you have more children?'

'That will never be. Too many seasons have passed.'

Jourbor hated to see his mother so unhappy, he wanted to cheer her up. So he moved closer to their visitor and said. 'Famous hunter, will you tell me a story?'

M'kama stroked his beard and said in a gruff voice. 'Only if you listen and learn from what I say.'

'Oh yes, I will. What is it about?' The boy's keen eyes shone, his brown complexion smooth and taut. In time Leena will cut the tribal marks above his temples symbolising his passage into adulthood.

'It's about how a man built his house.'

'A strong house like my mother's. She always builds our huts.'

M'kama held up his hand and said. 'Yes, strong as your mother's. Hush now and listen, no more questions.' The storyteller began:

Man and child lived on the edge of the jungle. Man built his house with straight strong tree trunks. He filled the gaps between the poles with red earth that hardened as it dried. He thatched the roof with tall golden grass held securely with vines. To protect his home and garden he fashioned a stockade from sturdy logs and left spaces at intervals from where he could shoot the wild threatening animals. He was safe.

White termites built their hilly homes beside his house. Baboons tried to scale the stockade but man warded

32

them off with his arrows. Many rhinoceroses tried to break down the enclosure with their heavy bodies. The logs were too strong. At night the hippopotami left their muddy pools. They craved the flourishing vegetables in the garden. All the beasts were unsuccessful in their attempt to get in.

The termites' houses grew taller.

Leopards coughed and circled the stockade. And the lion's roar shook the earth telling all he was the king of the forest. Child cried, but man told him not to be afraid. They were safe.

Termites continued to build their houses.

In the moonlight the hyenas howled. Close by wild dogs barked and snarled.

Man and child lived securely for three years. Then the house collapsed and the stockade fell down. The termites had eaten through all the logs. The wild beasts rushed in and demolished the garden and ate up man and child.

'Well,' said M'kama, 'what did you learn from that story?'

'Little creatures cause trouble, I think,' said Jourbor.

M'kama laughed. 'Well, you are nearly right. It also tells us to look around us. Kangera. Kangera. Observe. Watch out for the small creatures that can harm you.' M'kama stood and raised his spear. 'I must go now.'

'May I go a little way with you, Uncle?' asked Jourbor respectfully.

'If your mother allows it.'

'Yes, but only to the edge of the forest,' said Leena and the friends touched hands. M'kama the hunter, storyteller and poet, turned his back and went on his way. The small naked boy trotted behind him.

Although the sun had passed its highest point, the heat still lingered. Leena washed her saucepan in the stream and tethered the goat closer to the hut. She stooped under the zebra skin that covered the doorway of the second hut. Lying on her mat, she laughed to herself. Gods rising from big, very big waters, digging holes in the ground and eating sweet

33

sand, what fairy tales she thought. Content in her Stone Age world, Leena fell asleep.

In time she would draw water from white man's well. She did not believe that he was a minor god, for he had red hair. Jourbor, her only child, would straddle the centuries. Her grandchildren would never experience her reality. She lived in a past era and thought little of the present. But one idea carried her into the twentieth century: it was the notion of wearing a head-dress, soft as thistledown like the seventh colour of the rainbow.

M'kama and Jourbor skirted the long grass at the edge of the forest. They walked in a single file, stopping occasionally to spear large field mice foraging in the grass. Plaiting their tails together M'kama attached them on his belt. They'd make a reasonable supper.

'What do you see?' M'kama asked Jourbor as they resumed their journey.

The boy looked about and shook his head. 'I see the sun and clouds and trees. There are the broad-leafed cacti that mother uses for rope.'

'See that tree that stands alone. It is waving to us. It's the friendly tree.'

'Yes, I see now. There isn't much wind, yet leaves are fluttering. How do they do that?'

'If you look carefully, you'll see the bottom leaves on the stem are the largest. They flutter in the slightest breeze.'

Jourbor jumped up and down. 'Yes, now I understand. I must look, be observant.'

Quiet rustling in the grass cautioned them of a column of black army ants. The insects were on the march to the termite hill. Both hikers stepped warily over the cavalcade.

Jourbor studied the habitat. He saw drongos flitting above the grass. Their forked tails dipped and rose gracefully as the birds snatched at flying insects. He heard the cry of the lonely jackal, a yearning howl from the other side of the hill.

Jourbor looked up and down, to the right and left but not in front. Until he collided into M'kama's buttocks. The hunter had stopped in his stride. Slowly, he raised his arm, opened his shoulders and braced his body. With his spear well back he poised to throw. Jourbor peeped around the hunter's legs and saw Hattie asleep under the msasa tree. The whites of his eyes, large as the wild loquats, bulged from their sockets.

'No! Uncle, no. It's the river god's child,' whispered the boy staring at the figure below him. It looked very white as if recently washed. Maybe it had risen out of the river. It had a scar on the leg, shaped like the forked tail of the drongo. It was a blemish he'd always remember. Jourbor blinked. He didn't believe what he saw. The soles of the tiny feet had brown leathery flesh attached to them. Skin that may be removed.

He tugged on M'kama's pants, and pointed. '. . . Look there, the elephant's spoor. Elephants . . . close by.' This was too much for the small lad. He swung around and bolted the way he had come. The last M'kama saw of him was a little brown body darting between the cacti and boulders, the string of lucky beans flapping around his belly.

M'kama lowered his spear and stepped up noiselessly to take a closer look. Jourbor had been right. There was elephant spoors around the white god child.

'It *has* skinny legs.' He bent over and peered into the little pallid face. It's quite pretty and it has a winsome quality about its form. Wonder if it's a male or female. Can't tell with that cloth wrapped around the legs? He stood back and rattled his carved shield against the long spear.

Hattie awoke and peeked from under her arm. Raising her head, she smiled and greeted him in a strange language. M'kama frowned ferociously, pounded his spear and rattled his shield and thought: This child has no manners. She spoke first and looked straight at him – he, the mighty hunter. He gave her another of his ferocious looks, scowling and drawing his lips across his strong white teeth. Unafraid, she smiled again.

This child is so brazen, M'kama decided, it must be a female. There is no harm in her for she is a lost child. A

35

child with charm, grace and innocence. Now what was he to do with her? He dared not leave as she'd be defenceless against the prowlers of the night. Was it his destiny to teach and rescue children? He, the brave hunter who killed the leopard. True, he found it in the ravine, old and sick with the vermin leaping from the dying carcass. True, it did bare its yellow teeth and look at him through pleading green eyes. M'kama, he, the fearless hunter speared the beast through the neck. The beast rose, threw out a paw. He jumped back, lifted his spear to strike again. The animal collapsed at his feet. The red blood burst all over him. M'kama told a good story.

With a jerk of his head he walked from the child. Hattie had no wish to remain alone so she jumped up and followed but kept a fair distance from the twitching rats at his waist.

Once along the trail, M'kama stopped. He placed his shield and spear on the ground and headed for a solitary tree. Wild loquats clustered under the leaves. He gathered a handful and placed them on the ground and walked on. Hattie picked up the fruit and bit into one. The bitter juice quenched her thirst.

As the afternoon edged into the evening, the white clouds changed from blue to pink. M'kama and Hattie plodded on until suddenly Hattie sensed more than saw the familiar surroundings. Yes, she realised she stood on the path leading to the river. To her left, among the wild marigolds, stood the old Model-T Ford. At the end of the path was her home, a crude structure of poles and mud. Hattie looked about for her deliverer to thank him. He had vanished.

Seth, forlorn and dejected, faced their mother by the cabbage patch. Three plants remained in the small bed. Miraculously the seeds had sprouted, as the soil lacked the necessary nutrients for alien plants. Yellowed and bent on thin stalks, the cabbages reached maturity. Sampling the lower leaves, the browsers and caterpillars disliked the vegetable and had moved on.

Hattie's mother held one yellowed plant by the stalk. Clods of black soil still clung to the roots. Her body was thin now.

36

Empty skin hung from the upper arms and folds of flesh sagged from her cheeks and neck.

'It's not right, children running wild,' she spoke severely pounding the air with the cabbage. 'Where have you been? It's late and where's Hattie. I haven't seen her for hours; I told you to mind her.'

Seth scraped his bare toes in the sand. 'I . . . I left her at the river.'

'Oh God, is she safe? The river, the flood.' Mrs Carver screamed. Dropping the cabbage, she grabbed Seth by the shoulders. 'I told you to mind her. Hattie! Hattie!'

Seth hid his face in his bent arm. He wailed. 'I'm sorry, so sorry. The water came rushing down, a huge wall of water. It scared me. I ran and left her . . . ran away.'

'It's all right Seth. I'm safe,' Hattie called from the edge of the path. 'I lost my way.'

Seth and his mother twisted around. The little girl ran down the path. Shafts of sunlight caught the metal on the old car and brightened the patch of marigolds. From deep within the woodlands Seth heard an emerald-spotted dove call above the anguish in his mother's voice.

'Oh Hattie, what happened to you? Alone and lost in the wilds.'

'I'm sorry . . .' Seth began but his mother's voice cut in.

'Why must we live like this, no proper food or suitable clothes? We have no friends or relations close by. You both need schooling. It's not right. We must leave here. We must leave now.'

Covering her face to hide her tears, Mrs Carver went into the primitive house followed by the two children. Later that night and unable to sleep, Hattie left her bed and went outside. The shrubs and trees stood motionless in the heat of the night. Her long calico nightdress disturbed a nest of scorpions from their rest as she climbed an outcrop of granite. So close were the stars that she held up her hands to touch them.

When the dew began to fall, she returned to the house. In the bedroom Seth lay, his limbs hung over the edge of the bed, sweat drenched his body. Hattie quietly crawled into her bed and drew the sheet to her chin and tried to sleep. Behind closed eyelids Hattie saw visions of paths, like branches of a tree that led into the darkness. Somewhere, out in the night a leopard coughed, a baboon screeched.

'We must leave,' the words pounded in her head, 'we are leaving. Where will we go?'

Chapter 4

The officer, standing against the ship's railings, glanced at an empty sleeve here, a bandaged eye there and a pair of crutches propped against a chair. He'd seen it all before, on a different ship, from a different war. Fragmented sentences spoken from the repatriated soldiers floated past him.

'Alma said he looked like me, he's four years old and I have never seen him.'

'Wait until I get . . .'

'Oh for a pint of bitter . . .'

The officer watched the breakers crash and die against the hull. They were followed by another and another in the monotonous movement of the sea. Sometimes the waves carried dark forms that swam on the crest then quickly sunk into the depth below.

A kitbag labelled, 'Lieut. William Auston-Jones' lay at the feet of a soldier who leaned over the railings and stared intently at the ocean. Thick brown hair hung over the broad forehead and arched brows. Expressions in the brown eyes changed from gentleness to cruelty as thoughts chased through his mind. The high-bridged nose accentuated soft lips and a square chin. Holding a crumpled letter in his long fingers, he bent as if mesmerised by the swells below him.

Lieutenant Auston-Jones mumbled aloud, 'Andy Anderson, my father's friend. Who'd be friends with my father? He dominated those around him, the old sod. I can't recall a Mr Andy Anderson, who wrote this letter. He says he saw

39

my painting. I remember the watercolour; my mother hung it in the passage, I wonder if it's still there?'

William pulled two gold medals from his pocket and studied them for a moment and continued his monologue. 'Oh, what's the use of these now. I wonder if I can whack one of those shadows if they come close to the hull.' He leaned still farther over the rail until a strong hand gripped his shoulder and he heard a quiet voice:

'Hold on old boy, you don't want to do that.'

Surprised at the firm hold on his shoulder, William whipped round to face the old officer. Except for a neatly pointed beard and thin lips, his other features were hidden under a peaked cap.

'What do you mean? What don't I want to do?' William asked aggressively.

'Jump overboard. You were going to jump.'

William relaxed and chuckled. 'No. I had no intention of doing away with myself. I was looking for the creatures in the water. Did you see them riding the wave?'

'Probably sharks or dolphins. We're sailing into the Tropics. You sounded depressed, heard you mumbling.'

'I always talk to myself. Never really had anyone to talk to.'

The officer pointed to the letter in William's hand. 'Have you received bad news from home?'

He shrugged. 'Yes . . . but it happened so long ago, almost three years when I was on the front line. The letter caught up with me recently while I was in the hospital.' William stared vaguely around and then softly repeated. 'It's all so unrelated and hard to believe.'

'What happened?'

'Father committed suicide because my sister disgraced the family name. She and a local man were living together.'

The officer gasped. 'Surely that's not a disgrace.'

'Oh yes it is. In the colonies it is taboo to associate with other races. The native's family also objected to the union, so his brother murdered the couple. My sister was Father's favourite child, a clever, beautiful young woman. Like Father, she rode a horse with style and courage. Her death and the humiliation shattered the old man. A stable boy found his body on Pioneer Hill which is close to the house. My aged mother is senile now and she lives in a mental home at the coast.'

The officer scrutinised the face before him. William's indifferent attitude only served to stress the pain that showed in his eyes. Here stood a man who had seen so much and yet knew nothing about life. A mere schoolboy pitched into the theatre of war. Courageously he had faced his adversities and now, in peacetime, this young-old man was apprehensive of the future.

'What a sad homecoming it will be for you,' he said raising his cap a few inches.

William saw straight dense eyebrows like eaves protecting two pale blue windows.

'Yes, of course,' he answered. 'I . . . suppose so, but then you never knew my parents. I'm their *big disappointment*. The runt of the brood who embarrassed them. My siblings, except my sister, succumbed to tropical diseases, yet I survived the usual children's illnesses and two bouts of malaria fever. "Willy the Wimp" my father called me because I continually sniffed with head colds and I hated horses. The bloody animals petrified me. My parents sent me to boarding school at a tender age. I must learn to be a man they told me.'

The learning institute in the old country that William attended specialised in discipline. 'Be a man,' the teachers encouraged the pupils. One day William said to his school prefect, a fellow student from the colonies:

'They said I must be a man but I'm only ten,' sobbed the lonely little boy.

'That "be a man" stuff is a crock of crap,' said Toss McPhearson and unwittingly his words influenced the lad. So the naïve William, intrigued with hard cs and the rolling rs, believed the headmaster would appreciate the sounds. Unfortunately, the headmaster thought differently. William's rear end hurt for weeks.

Holding out the medals to the officer, William continued: 'I wanted to show these to my father, prove to him I'm not such a wimp. Now it's too late.' William arched his arm back.

'No. Don't throw them away,' shouted the officer. 'One day you will show them to your sons.'

William lowered his arm, grimaced at the medals. 'Bah,' he said and stuffed them in his pocket.

'Your father, was a pioneer?'

'No, he was one of the early settlers.'

'Tell me about the country and the people.'

'I haven't been home for years yet remember it as a cruel, beautiful land of gentle rolling hills and valleys. A range of mountains rise in the east. They stand there as if to keep watch over the grasslands and forests. Most of the soil is fertile and the rocks are rich in minerals. There is a mixture of races, yet all are identified with the country. I don't know if the land influences the people or vice versa. The colony is a Protectorate. Probably, after some tragedy it will achieve independence. My father often quoted the famous words "so much to do so little done".' William's laughter was mirthless.

'My father and his colleagues were strong and idealistic. It's no wonder I'm a wimp in his eyes. All I did was paint and watch the wildlife. One day I'll be recognised for what I am.'

The ship creaked and rode another swell as the naval officer at William's side asked. 'Who is Andy Anderson?'

Poking the letter with his bony forefinger, William answered. 'My father's, sorry, late father's accountant. He tells me that I am a wealthy man. Mr Anderson invested my father's money in sound stock. He says he awaits my instructions and wants to welcome me home.' William gave the letter another jab. 'I guess I'll leave it all to this Mr Anderson. He's honest and capable. What the hell do I know about stocks and shares.'

The officer gave a dry cackle. 'That sounds like the right decision. What will you do with your life now?'

'Buy a car, a Jaguar. Yes, a white XJ6. Maybe I'll paint

42

and get so drunk at night that I'll forget the colours of war. I want to forget the reds from gaping mouths and the screams of agony above the bedlam. Maybe the pictures of the crimson-reds of blood spurting from opened chests will fade, and so might the yellows in the flames that changes to white as the artillery warheads exploded on target.'

The ship creaked, whispering secrets of bygone sailors as the hull churned through the sea. Dark greens, olives and emeralds coloured the breakers as they surged and withdrew on their way to nowhere. In the distance, sunlight stabbed through the low clouds. A ray burnished the crest of the waves, like a promise of brighter days. Suddenly the glowing faded.

'I'll acquire the taste for whisky; my mates tell me it's a gentleman's drink. I hate the bloody stuff but it might make me forget.'

The officer sniffed. 'What about women, will you marry?'

William shook his letter in panic and almost squeaked, 'Christ no! I want peace, had enough conflict in my life.'

'Oh! One will get you,' the officer moved away. 'It's the eyes that entice. A man always remembers a woman's eyes.'

'Bah!' came the reply.

The ship ploughed on through the breakers taking William home to the welcome of his late father's friend, Andy Anderson.

Tropical sunlight tumbled into the room as the servant set the tray on the bedside table and drew the curtains. William raised his head from the pillow. A pain stabbed through his head.

'Jesus!' he cursed, how much had he drunk last night? Did he finish the second bottle? He now almost enjoyed the taste of whisky. The golden liquid appealed to his sense of colour and the three-cornered bottle fitted comfortably in his hand. Besides, with all his inheritance he could afford it.

There were nights when the chaos and smells of conflict of battle were too vivid. No amount of liquor could block out the visions of reds and yellows and black stinking smoke.

43

On those nights William remained on the veranda, the only place he found a vestige of peace. Lying on a divan, he watched the stars travelling across the night sky. They helped ease the pain.

This morning his hangover proved that the drink had worked its sorcery. The room tilted as he swung his legs over the side of the bed. Supporting his head in his hands, he waited until the ache settled somewhere at the back of his head. Muttering all the profanities he knew, he slowly stood up and cursed again: 'Bloody sunlight.'

Dressed in his robe, William passed four empty bedrooms and shambled down the staircase. At the bottom of the steps he paused to glance to the left.

'Must get rid of this place,' he muttered. 'Why do I need passages, leading this way and that. This house with all its lounges, stone pillars and circular driveways, is like a bloody temple.' He ran his fingers through his hair and added, 'Bloody Persian rugs under the dining-room table. Waste of money, who needs them.'

At the kitchen door he grunted a greeting to his household staff and entered the dining-room. William stopped in front of a portrait and raised two fingers in mock salute.

'You old bastard. Why do I always come back? Three years of travelling since the war and yet I always return. Why?' he asked the unsmiling face as he picked up a letter from the table and read it through twice.

'Bloody income tax,' he cursed aloud and charged out the room and down the passage. His robe flapped about his ankles.

An hour later, William stalked into the accountant's office.

'Where's Anderson?' he demanded of a young girl at the counter. She stared into his brown eyes. A smile dimpled her cheeks.

'What is the trouble, Hattie?' a voice called out.

'Mr Anderson, this gentleman has . . .'

A weathered brown face appeared around the door. 'William. Hello, my boy. Always good to see you, come into my office.'

44

That evening, with his chin resting on his hand and staring at the golden liquor through the cut glass, William deliberated. 'Should I see her again? Might be amusing.' He pinched his bottom lip and remembered the girl, Hattie, at the office. The girl with the smoky eyes, light blue or lilac? That old naval officer knew something about women. It's the woman's eyes that captivated a man. Should he see her again?

Chapter 5

'William has suddenly taken a lively interest in his finances,' remarked Andy Anderson to his wife. The elderly couple sat companionably in front of the fire. Not often did they need such a luxury, but the winter had been unusually cold. 'He came to the office for the fourth time in as many days.'

Mrs Anderson chuckled. 'Really! Men are so blind. Are you sure his preoccupation is with his ledgers?'

'Yes. What else?'

'Hattie Carver?'

'Definitely not. She slights him and is almost rude to him. Why the other morning when I arrived at the office, she was telling him to leave. Said she was busy and didn't expect me in until later.'

'No girl wants to be courted in an office.'

'William Auston-Jones courting? Never. He's too idle, content enough to procrastinate.' Andy thought for a moment before adding in a quieter tone, 'And is more concerned with his own comforts.'

Mrs Anderson frowned and made her decision. 'We'll invite William, Hattie and several young people for a barbecue. Give the couples a chance to meet and get to know each other. I'll tip off our other friends. I'm sure they will organise other activities.'

'My dear, I'm surprised. I didn't know you were a matchmaker,' laughed Andy. 'Do you think William is the right man for Hattie? I'm afraid he drinks too much. He may hurt her in some way. I wouldn't like anything nasty to happen to her. He needs someone strong and dominant at his side, a person to encourage and support his artist's talents.'

'That's understandable. Poor lad, he never had much of a childhood, with his parents busy leading social lives and fussing with keeping up with their traditions. How much did he suffer during the war? Has he ever told you about his war experiences?'

'No. He keeps that bottled up and that concerns me. He might vent his frustrations on a naïve girl.'

'Don't you believe that Hattie is so naïve. Remember she has that red-headed brother who watches over her like a mother hen.'

'You're right. It's the least we can do for William. Put some meaning into his life. Why do I feel like his surrogate father?'

Mrs Anderson laughed. 'It is your compassionate looks. Most youngsters want to cuddle up to you.'

'William is the last person I want cuddling up to me.'

Mrs Anderson's requests to her friends brought a flurry of house parties and other forms of entertainment. Several young couples met, paired off and later became engaged to be married. Two months later William phoned Hattie.

'Come to my home for dinner, you'll be safe,' he said. 'I'm harmless really.'

Hattie laughed. 'Thank you but I can't.'

William replied bluntly. 'You are staying with Rona Bentwood, aren't you? I'll fetch you at four. We dress for dinner.' He replaced the receiver.

The ringing of the doorbell disturbed Rona Bentwood from her afternoon's siesta. Placing her book on the arm of the chair, she stood up. She was a tall woman, with a squared body and thin legs. Her fine grey hair was neatly pinned at the nape of her neck. Glancing in the wall mirror, she adjusted her tweed skirt, tweaked at the hem of her blue cardigan and satisfied with her appearance, she answered the ring.

48

William, dressed in immaculate white drill, stood at the door. He faced Rona, his one hand in his pocket, the other smacking his cloth hat against his thighs.

'Good afternoon, is Hattie in? I told her I'd fetch her at four,' he said.

Rona looked him up and down before answering. 'Yes. She's in the garden. It's only just gone three-thirty.'

'I'm early because I want you to do something for me.'

He explained quickly, twisting the hat around and around in his fists. Rona looked dubiously at him and frowned. 'I'm not sure Hattie would agree,' she said.

William compressed his lips and lowered his head. 'Please do this favour for me.'

'Very well, but I'm not to blame if Hattie is annoyed,' Rona said relenting. 'Give me a few minutes then I'll tell her she has a visitor.'

'Thanks. I'll wait by the jeep,' replied William as he plunked his hat on his head.

Rona glanced at the old jeep standing in the driveway. What a horrible vehicle to court a young woman in.

'You drive a Jag, don't you?'

For an answer William nodded and winked.

Hattie came running lightly down the passage twenty minutes later. She stopped at the front door and looked disappointedly at William. He stood nonchalantly against the cab of the jeep.

'Rona told me someone was waiting for me, I thought it was Seth,' she said.

'Who is Seth?' asked William petulantly.

Hattie disregarded the question. 'I told you. I can't have dinner with you. I'm busy this afternoon.'

William held out his hand to her. 'Yes, I know, but please Hatts, come with me. I want to show you something.'

Hattie heard the intensity in his voice and no one had ever called her 'Hatts' before. She rather liked it.

'Very well, but you'll bring me home early.'

'Any time you wish.'

'Come in while I change my clothing.'

49

'No need for you to change, your skirt and blouse will be fine,' said William. He glanced at her slim ankles. 'Your runners are ideal for walking. Come.' He held the car door open for her.

'This is an ideal vehicle for game viewing. Do you visit the game parks?' remarked Hattie as they set off.

'Yes, I go there quite often. You don't mind riding in this jeep? It's pretty old.'

'Heavens no! Seth drives an old rattle-trap.'

Damn this Seth, William muttered under his breath. Before they reached the turn-off to his estate, William pulled over to the edge of the road.

'There is a path beyond the trees. To the right, it leads to the marketplace,' he said pointing, 'and to the left it ends at the house. Pioneer Hill is that way. Let's walk.'

Hattie followed William until they came to a white and red trimmed stable. The riding school lay hushed as if expecting a child to turn a key and start the action. Empty stalls silently waited for the clatter of ponies' hooves and children's voices. Hattie opened the door and looked into the clean and tidy stalls. Gleaming leather saddles and bridles lay on wooden trestles waiting for young riders.

Gently Hattie closed the door and joined William by the railings.

'Look past the broken fence – I must mend it one of these days, you can just see the jacaranda in bloom,' said William.

'It's beautiful. Is that what you wanted to show me?'

'N . . . No. Would you like to climb the hill?' he asked hurriedly. 'There is a better view from there.'

They reached the summit and Hattie pointed to a high building in the distance. 'Andy's office is in that building. Who built that huge house down there?'

'That's my place. A pioneer built part of it and my father added extra rooms. He installed the hot water system. The old boiler at the back still serves the servants' quarters and the kitchen. You might just see it from here.'

'Is it one of those boilers made from petrol drums set up on bricks?'

50

'Yes,' laughed William. 'I'm sure years ago every household had one.'

'This was a small community then.'

'That's right, before the First World War. Once this house stood in the centre of the town. Pioneer Hill served as a lookout for marauding tribes. The city has grown east, beyond the cemetery. My grandparents, father, brother and a sister are buried there.'

Which member of the family shall lie there next? The question slipped through William's mind. For a moment he sat dejectedly before continuing.

'My mother came from a well-connected family. Her trousseau contained silver and chinaware. She had the trees planted along the driveway and planned the garden. Dahlias are her favourite flowers.'

'Mine too,' interrupted Hattie.

'... she upheld all the old traditions and hosted many official functions.'

'Where is your mother now?'

'She lives at the coast. Poor dear is quite senile and doesn't recognise me now.'

'That's very sad. Do you live alone?'

'Quite alone. After the war I travelled a lot, but always returned. Every day I threatened to either sell the place or pull it down. Let us go down now, it's time for tea.'

'This view, is this what you wanted to show me?'

'Hm ... no. I'll tell you later. Come, we'll go back to the house,' he repeated.

After tea that awaited them in the front lounge, William led her to the side veranda. She sat on the step, her arms around her bare legs while he stretched out on the divan, supporting his weight on his forearm.

'That post against the garage, what's it for?' she asked.

'A hitching post for my bike. I pretended it was a horse. I hated live horses. It's a wonder it's there after all these years. Other children may use it one day,' he added quietly.

Hattie shrugged as if she didn't hear. 'I can't ride a bike, never owned one.'

51

She touched the petal of the honeysuckle that rambled over the railing. During the days the roots kept the soil moist and warm, a suitable habitat for earthworms and a multitude of crawling insects. Lead-green leaves and blossoms sheltered a variety of tiny wildlife and their predators.

'That scar on your leg, what happened?' William asked.

Hattie rubbed the forked blemish on her calf. 'Years ago I cut myself on barbed wire. I was always in trouble.'

'Tell me about your childhood.'

'There is not much to tell. I haven't seen or visited any exciting places or done anything remarkable like you.'

'Tell me.'

Hattie related incidents of her childhood and ended by saying. 'The day after my dunking in the river we left. Shame! My poor brother, he has never forgiven himself for leaving me at the river. He is forgiven, I've said so often, yet he still lives with the guilt. One day he tells me, he will make it up to me. Anyhow, Ma packed our few belongings in the black tin trunk. I loathed that trunk – I had the most dreadful dreams about it. Dear God, how I dislike cabbage. Cabbage and corn porridge, that's all we had to eat. Don't laugh.'

'I never have cabbage for dinner or porridge for breakfast. Where's the trunk now?'

'I couldn't say, maybe Seth has it at his farm.'

William rose from the divan to fetch a drink from a nearby table.

'Who is Seth?' William asked as he sat down.

Hattie hid her laugh. 'Don't look so outraged. Seth is my brother. He has a big red beard and the bluest eyes I've ever seen.'

'Oh . . . your brother. I'll have to meet him sometime. Go on, what happened next?'

'Yes, you must meet him. The following day after the flood, Ma drove Seth and me to Fort Briggs in the old Model-T Ford. That was about 1933.'

'What happened to your father?'

'He went crazy with the gold fever. We never saw him again. Over the years news filtered back. Some said he went

52

to live with a tribe in the interior. Other prospectors came back with stories of human bones scattered about that area.'

Hattie placed her chin on her knees. 'At Fort Briggs, we lived on charity for years. Seth and I went to school. He joined the forces, spent all the war years in the desert. Ma worked at several menial jobs, then one day she died. Just like that,' Hattie clicked her fingers, 'completely spent. Without proper food and medicine her health deteriorated.'

William twisted the crystal goblet of golden liquid, yet untouched, in his long fingers. 'How did you manage on your own?'

'Lived in the orphanage. When I was seventeen or so I came here to Ashvale and Mr Anderson gave me a job. That's where I first saw you. Remember? You came bounding into the office like the dominant gorilla who had lost his harem to a juvenile.'

After spluttering and choking with laughter William said, 'You'll . . . pay . . . for that remark, my girl.'

Hattie changed the subject. 'Where's the boundary of your estate?'

William turned and pointed over a privet hedge. 'All the land to the highway belongs to the estate. Africans are using my property as a short cut. So many of them are drifting into the city. It's this call for independence that's making them restless.'

'I've noticed many come from the area where I lived.' She glanced at a pond in the centre of the lawn. 'Are there fish in there?'

'No, frogs live in it now. We tried to keep goldfish but the kingfishers nabbed them.' William stretched back on the divan. 'On clear nights I sleep out here, and this,' he said, lifting a covering beyond his head, 'is Grandmother's patchwork quilt. It's quite warm.' He pinched his bottom lip to stop an impudent smile.

Embarrassed by a thought that crossed her mind, Hattie mumbled. 'Do . . . you . . . farm the land?'

'I have a very competent manager. He takes care of the estate. I spend most of my time painting.'

'Portraits?'

'No, I paint what I see before me, a bird's feather and curling leaves. Some day I'd like to do a portrait of a beautiful woman. I haven't found a model yet.'

'Well, I'm safe from your brush,' Hattie smiled.

William sat up, leaned forward and gently lifted her chin. With unusually still eyes, he scrutinised her features.

'Dear Hatts, no one could ever portray your grace. Maybe one day I might try to capture the lilac and the compassion in your eyes.'

'William, you're a romantic,' Hattie answered and withdrew from his touch.

'Romantic! First I'm a gorilla and now a romantic.'

Nonchalantly, his companion tossed his words back. 'Hm . . . A gorilla, romantic or not, yes you could be one. Like the apes, you have bony wrists, strong hands and fidgety eyes. Your ancestors might have roamed the hills. Your hair is the colour of a roan antelope, reddish-brown. The auburn brightens when sunlight catches it. I once saw a roan antelope from a train window. It stood majestically against the skyline.'

'My men and fellow officers referred to me in many uncomplimentary terms. Yet never was I called a randy ape with red-brown hair. Do you always compare men to animals?'

'Quite often. I think Mr Anderson looks like a turtle, especially when he pokes his head around the door.'

'I'll remember to tell him that.'

William stood up and emptied his glass of golden liquid over the railings. It really was true, he thought. It is the eyes that lure and capture men.

The honeysuckle slowly opened its slender petals, offering moonmoths its fragrant desserts. A caterpillar crawled to the end of the leaf and stretched over the void. Poised, it swayed searching for hold, oblivious of a chameleon close by. The creature with baggy green skin rolled its protruding eyes independently. The left eye caught the movement of the caterpillar, the right eye rolled its pupil into focus. Curling its tail

54

around the branch for support, the mouth opened. A gooey tongue shot out to snatch. It missed the target and the caterpillar fell to the ground. Unwinding its tail, the predator went looking for another meal.

Hattie saw the movement in the honeysuckle. 'Oh look, a visitor. Chameleons are such mysterious creatures. Most Africans are afraid of them. They believe they are evil spirits reincarnate.'

Hattie placed her foot on the step below her, it teetered precariously.

'Be careful of that step,' William cautioned. 'I must fix it one of these days.'

She reached down for a twig and lifted the chameleon.

'That creature will bite you,' William said.

'It won't. I once kept them as pets, until my mother found them under the bed – she threw them out.'

'Quite understandable. Don't you let that creature into my house.'

'Look at the rippling of his muscles as he sways backwards. His tail is the correct length to balance his body. He changes colour when he climbs on to my hand. Would you like to hold him?'

'Heavens above, no. My dear Hatts, I didn't bring you here for a nature lesson.'

'You should know more about nature in this country than me. You were born here. I'm a transplant, like the jacaranda.'

'I spent my childhood in boarding school outside the country, learning how to be a gentleman.'

'And I, in the bush, learning how to survive,' Hattie said. 'See the chameleon roll one eye, just like this.'

Hattie raised her brows, closed one eye and rolled the other.

William chuckled. 'That's nothing like the chameleon. Your eyes are lilac. You haven't answered my question. Are you unafraid of all the creatures you collect?'

'No.'

'Are you afraid of people?'

'N . . . no. Not really, just shy.'

55

'Shy of me?'

Hattie started to shake her head. 'Maybe a little.'

The chameleon climbed onto the twig. Hattie stood up and walked to the jacaranda tree. She propped the twig against the tree and went back to the step.

'The clouds above Pioneer Hill are changing into candyfloss,' she whispered.

Candyfloss clouds became a golden coastline in the sea of the evening sky. William stood up and held out his hand to Hattie. He guided her across the veranda to the screen door and took her in his arms. Silhouetted against the setting sun, he kissed her.

'William, you said you wanted to show me something.' Hattie pulled away from him.

'Yes. Come upstairs to the bedroom and I'll show you.'

Chapter 6

William opened the bedroom door and stood aside to let Hattie enter. She hesitated, frowning at him.

'It's okay. I said you could trust me.'

Hattie went into the room and glanced about her. 'What a delightful bedroom. Who sleeps here?' William shrugged.

Russet-coloured curtains complemented the handsome rosewood furniture and bedlinen. A silver grey wall-to-wall carpet added a final touch of luxury. On the bed lay her evening skirt and blouse. Her overnight case was on the chair.

'William, my clothing. How did it get there?'

'The tooth-fairy, in the form of Rona Bentwood, sent them. There's time to bathe and dress. Dinner will be ready in thirty minutes.' He turned and walked quickly down the stairs.

After bathing and dressing, Hattie brushed her brown hair to curl under her chin.

'That'll have to do,' she said to her reflection in the mirror and left the room.

William, in evening dress, met her at the bottom of the steps. He drew her close.

'How lovely you are, captivating and charming,' he said and kissed her lips. From his jacket pocket he drew out a flawless diamond clasp.

'This belonged to my grandmother. I want you to have it.' He said and pinned it to her blouse. 'My grandfather mined these diamonds somewhere in South Africa, they were the only ones he found.'

'William! They're . . . so beautiful.'

He smiled, kissed her again and escorted her to the dining-room. An arrangement of dahlias filled the corner of the room and in the centre of the table a silver vase held three perfect blooms. Hattie gasped. 'The flowers, how gorgeous they are!'

Behind Hattie's back, William flicked his opened fingers at his father's sharp features and small beady eyes which were paralysed for ever in oil paints.

With Hattie seated on his right, William raised his glass to salute her.

'Welcome, Hattie.' She acknowledged his welcome with a naughty smile in her eyes.

Hattie ate her food with enjoyment but refused second helpings. For dessert, a crystal bowl of strawberries was set in front of her.

'William, strawberries are out of season. Where do these come from?'

'Imported. There's a small shop on Main Street that specialises in imported food.'

Questions like bubbles in boiling water rose to her lips as their eyes met. Later, much later she would know the answers. She reached over and slipped her hand into his. 'How thoughtful, and sensitive you are. I'm honoured and flattered. Thank you.'

William raised her fingers to his lips and later with his arm around her waist they returned to the veranda. As the evening became cool, the sky brightened with starlight, William led Hattie down the steps, carefully minding the second one.

Around the garden they began to dance. Slowly at first, then faster and faster they capered. Fireflies circled above the couple's heads in a frantic dance of their own. In the fish-pond a bullfrog raised her head. Her mate croaked his love song accompanied by a barn owl hooting from a branch in the jacaranda tree. Nocturnal animals stopped their foraging and watched from shadowy places.

Hattie leaned away from William, her hair swirling around her face as they rollicked in a dance of their own. Around the fish-pond and back to the steps they danced. There they stopped.

'Will you marry me, Hatts?'

'Yes. If I can bring wild creatures into your house?'

William shook his head.

They danced again around the pond and back to the steps.

'If I painted pictures of your wildlife and hung them in the house, would you marry me?'

Hattie tilted her head, smiled and did not answer. They danced again around the garden, until Hattie stopped him at the steps.

'Will you allow babies into your house? Your babies,' she said. 'So one day they'll use the hitching post for their bikes.'

William threw back his head and laughed loudly. 'You heard and I thought you were shy. You hot little b . . .'

Hattie pulled his head down and kissed him hard on the lips. Twice more they danced around the garden. At the bottom of the steps, he undid her blouse and slipped off her clothing and she helped him off with his clothing. Lifting her in his arms he carried her up the steps and laid her on the divan.

Their love-making began. Enraptured in physical nearness and the blending of spirits, time passed by. At the witching hour they slowly floated back to earth.

In the garden, one by one the fireflies curled their delicate wings and muted their light. The bullfrogs gave a satisfied croak and sunk into the warmth of their muddy bed. Cuddled beneath his grandmother's patchwork quilt, William caressed Hattie with sensitive hands. Laying her head on his naked chest, she heard his heart beating strongly. It belonged to her.

'When must I take you home?' There was a smile in William's voice.

For an answer Hattie cuddled close.

A short time later, she murmured. 'William, what *did* you want to show me?'

'You've seen it, my darling. You've seen it all.'

The night became tranquil. All nature's children bedded down in warm and cosy beds. The owl, he stretched his wings and flew across the face of the noon.

A month later two men measured each other with misgivings. After Hattie had introduced Seth to her future husband, they began planning her wedding. Seth stroked his red beard in agitation. William glared every so often at the huge man sitting at the table.

'I'll drive you to the church in the Model-T Ford,' said Seth giving his beard an extra hard tug.

'Is that old car still in existence?' said Hattie.

'Yes. It's in perfect running condition.'

'Use the Chevy, or Jag. No woman wants to ride to her wedding in a vehicle that's so old,' insisted William. He resented Seth's domineering attitude, wanting to drag Hattie to her wedding in some old rattletrap. Who did he think he was, Hattie's guardian angel? I'm not good enough for her? William clamped his jaw, his temper rising. He had controlled battalions during the war and now he had no intention of taking any balderdash from this red-headed farmer. Seth looked William straight in the eye. He wasn't about to give his sister to some wealthy upstart. What had William accomplished in life? Okay! So he fought in the war. So what? I also gave five years of my life, Seth thought. All this mamsy-pamsy does is loll about squandering his time and money. Has he no ambition? He thinks he is some lord of the manor! Ordering people about. Once before he, Seth, had let Hattie down. Never will she be left again to face another crisis alone. He didn't trust this fellow with his beloved sister. She, his only family.

Hattie's brother and husband-to-be glared at each other. Hackles rising, swords were drawn, one waiting for the other to back down.

'You won't say where you're going for your honeymoon.

I suppose it's some fancy joint, somewhere to show off your conquest,' said Seth to annoy his future brother-in-law. Come on you pansy, let's see you fight.

William placed his hands on the table and slowly rose. No man spoke like that to him.

'You b . . .' He began.

'Stop it both of you,' Hattie demanded, 'you're like two bantam roosters sparring over a hen. William don't frown so. You're not about to order your men into battle. And you Seth, mind your manners. This is what we will do. You, Seth, my beloved brother, will drive me in your first love, that ridiculous old car. You, my dear darling William, shall take me away in your Jag.' Hattie supported her chin in her hands. 'Please tell me where we are to spend our honeymoon.'

'No,' said William. To resist the mischievous smile in her eyes he glanced down at the ill-fitting sweater that he wore. Lovingly he smoothed it down.

Seth peered at the garment and commented. 'Did Hattie knit that for you? It's hideous. Obviously she has never knitted anything in her life. I don't know why you want to marry her. She's not in the least domesticated.'

'I can bake bread,' chipped in Hattie.

'Okay I'll give you that, but a man can't live on bread alone.' Seth laughed and ducked as Hattie reached to whack him.

William's muttering stopped their banter.

'It's not obnoxious. It's warm and soft.' He pursed his lips and looked down at his chest. Again he rubbed his palms over the sweater. 'No one has ever made me anything before. It is very comfortable and I don't want to marry a domestic. I have enough servants.' He met Seth's gaze, daring him to criticise.

'You must really be in love with Hattie if you are willing to wear that! What colour is it? It looks like a baby's po . . .'

'Seth! That's enough,' said Hattie and held out her hand to William. He caressed it and they became lost in each other's loving eyes.

Seth bent his head, mixed emotions surging through his

61

mind. He had to lose his sister sometime. Hattie had found her love but would William cherish her?

From the steeple wedding bells rang out the good news. The choir and the congregation raised their voices in praise. No deafening silence on this happy occasion. The preacher held up his hands and blessed the young couple. He asked God to grant Hattie and William peace and happiness and healthy children.

Andy Anderson had the honour of standing up for William.

'What a lovely couple,' said Mrs Anderson at the ceremony and wiped the tears from her eyes.

'I sincerely hope Hattie is the right woman for him. William is still so unsettled.' Andy Anderson sighed.

'She is perfect for him. I have never seen a more suited couple. Have you noticed he's stopped drinking?'

The wedding feast took place in the garden on William's estate. Under colourful marquees the tables were set with fine crockery and silver cutlery. Guests mingled, admiring the setting. The ladies wore their finery and gentlemen were uncomfortably warm in top hat and tails.

Mrs Betsy Montecland donned her blue gown and picture hat. The stiffened lace trim fluttered as she bobbed her small head. She smiled continuously, stretching her thin upper lip over protruding teeth. Charlie, her spouse, was a well rounded man. The eyes were perfect circles in a spherical face and his neatly rounded head sat comfortably on his plump body. His stomach wobbled as he bounced from one spot to another. He greeted his friends in a high-pitched voice. 'Splendid, splendid,' and shook hands all round and bounced away.

Mrs Rona Bentwood sat close to the wedding feast with folded arms under her mature bosom. Eyeing each passerby, she evaluated their apparel and eavesdropped on their conversations. Several guests spoke to her. Many came to thank her for some favour. She nodded graciously and asked after their health and their family. Carefully, she stored all the information in the back of her mind. Later that night she'd mull over each morsel and file it for future reference. One never knew when such knowledge would be useful.

His Excellency, the ambassador, made a hurried visit. To William, he expressed his congratulations; to the bride he wished his felicitations and kissed her cheek.

Passersby of all sizes gathered along the broken fence. Some of the onlookers had just arrived from the interior. Their woolly heads appeared like cut-outs silhouetted against the skyline. Eyes widened when they saw the colourful dress of the wedding guests. In astonishment they exclaimed. 'These are the white gods!'

'A famous hunter rescued one from the elephant,' whispered a wide-eyed girl, 'my uncle told me.'

'Rubbish,' exclaimed a city dweller who was a smart dresser. He wore a jacket with leather patches on the sleeves, black pants, green shirt and flowing checked tie. 'They're not gods. They're crazy white folk. One day we'll live in their big houses.'

'Like that strange-shaped building?'

'Yes. It is a square house.'

'What is square?'

City dweller looked about him. Round tree trunks, round stones, oval clouds. There was nothing naturally square.

'It's a shape like this.' He formed a square with his fingers – the onlookers shrugged.

'. . . Never mind, you won't understand,' he muttered, 'you know nothing.'

A tinkling sound drifted over.

'What's that?'

'Ice in the glasses.'

'Ice?' The newcomers shook their heads. What was he talking about and why was he slowly edging to the back entrance of the house? City dweller knew the ways of white men. Strangers shared the leftovers; he wanted to be the first in line.

Newcomer climbed the jacaranda tree and shouted down.

63

'Who's the man holding on to the skinny woman? His hair is the colour of the bark of the msasa tree.'

'That's the groom,' answered City dweller.

'Why has he got that silly grin on his face?'

'You would grin too if you had just taken a bride.'

'Did he give many goats for her?' inquired Newcomer from the tree.

'Not many, I bet. She too skinny,' said Shoko, M'kama the hunter's wife, to her squint-eyed daughter. 'Come, Gladys, we must get to the market and set up our stall.' Gladys lifted a bag of produce onto her head and followed her mother.

'A white man doesn't buy his bride.'

'How many wives do the white men keep?'

'Only one at a time. Some of them share wives.' City dweller scratched his head.

'They're not like us, the men must be very weak,' decided an old man.

All the guests dancing to the strange music drew comments from the onlookers. 'Are they fighting? Why are they hugging each other while standing up? All that cloth must get in the way.'

At the reception, Seth angrily pulled William aside. He pointed to a sallow individual. 'Who is that bastard pouring whisky down his thin neck? He'll drink himself to oblivion. Is he a friend of yours? I don't want Hattie mixed up with the likes of him.'

'Hold on old man, calm down,' urged William.

'Well, who is he. He looks like a dope addict.'

'Toss McPhearson. I seldom see him now, maybe once or twice a year. He is a reprobate.' William laughed. 'Normally by this time of day he is mindless with the marijuana he chews. Most likely grows the stuff in his backyard. He enlightens me with the realities of life.'

'Are you friends with him?' Seth insisted.

'Sort of – he was my prefect at Kingsfield.'

'That toffee-nosed school!'

'Yes. There they told us one day we must be men. What

the hell else they thought we'd grow up to be, I never could fathom.'

Seth guffawed and pulled at his beard.

'Unfortunately, I'm forever indebted to old Toss,' William said. 'You see, at school he taught me my first curse words. My backside smarted for weeks, thanks to him.'

'What happened?'

'He told me that Kipling's poem "If" was a crock of crap. I innocently repeated that to my headmaster.'

'Why didn't they expel you?'

'Don't really know. Maybe because of my pretty face, and I did sing in the choir. Good old Toss – I never did know his real name. He's gone "native" as they say and has several wives. The light-skinned kids one sees around here are probably his.' William gave Seth a brotherly pat on the back. 'Don't concern yourself. Your beloved sister will be protected from his kind.' He moved off to find his bride.

William found her dressed in her going-away costume. As the guests waved and wished them well, he helped her into the Jaguar.

'Where are we going?' she asked again. He just winked and started the car. Through the city and countryside they went. Two hours later they stopped at a country hotel for the night. Hattie hesitated at the entrance of the hotel.

'Look William. Look over there,' she called to him over her shoulder.

He grimaced. 'Please Hattie, not another of your pet creatures?'

'N . . . No. I'm not sure what it is. It's not alive, never has been.'

William came up carrying their overnight bags. 'Where?'

Hattie pointed. 'There at the end of the garden. What is that stone statue, a bird or an angel?'

'I couldn't say. Whatever it is, it looks bloody constipated.'

'William,' she stressed, 'you are . . .'

'I know. I know. Come, my sweetheart, let's book in for the night. Then we do what the Good Book tells us to do. We'll begin to multiply.'

'William!'

They resumed their journey late the next morning. In the early afternoon they saw in the distance jets of vapour rising high above the msasa trees.

William stopped the car on the brow of the hill. 'There,' he said, 'is where we are to spend our honeymoon, my sweet.'

'A waterfall that sounds like smoking thunder. It is the most idyllic place on this earth,' Hattie said and gently kissed her husband.

As the nomads, pioneers, and a miscreant or two admired the waterfalls so did Hattie and William. The young married couple stood hand-in-hand and became oblivious to all but the grandeur before them. To their left, the water flowed deceptively calm but under that placid surface the current raged. Faster and faster it surged until, in a flurry of excitement, the breathing, heaving mass cascaded into a chasm below. Water slammed against the black rocks to form a savage whirlpool. Through deep and narrow gorges the current flowed. Released at last from the imprisonment, it meandered through the mahogany forests. Through woodlands and meadows until the waters reached the ocean and became fragmented in eternity.

Chapter 7

Through the cool early dawn, African women came from over the hills. With grace and poise they walked, balancing baskets of produce on their heads. Tied snugly on their backs their babies sleep soundly, comforted by the rhythm of swaying hips. Older children skipped and ran to keep up with their mothers' long strides. Down the hill, following the narrow path, the marketeers came in a single file. They mingled with the traffic on the main dusty road. Cycles, donkeys carrying bundles of hay, and hand-pushed carts snarled the oncoming traffic.

In the market the merchants arranged their wares on improvised tables. Enclosed in nature's wrappings, produce lay in tidy rows; fresh green corn, red tomatoes dulled with dust. The watermelons, protected in their shiny black and green striped skins, were piled under the tables. From the awnings, women hung dehydrated rodents and cuts of venison. Exotic fruit and wild berries for sale provided proteins, vitamins, medications and laxatives.

A toothless hag yelled at a passerby. 'Isaac, son of M'kama, you owe me money. When are you going to pay me? You have enough money to buy smart suits, red ties and silk shirts. All you ever do is to dress like a peacock and cause trouble with our employers.'

'You'll get your money, old mother,' Isaac answered.

'What did you learn at school, nothing but how to talk? I'll tell your father, the famous hunter, about you when he comes to visit.'

67

That's right, thought Isaac. At school I soon learned to tell the teachers what they wanted to hear. Avoiding the strewn garbage, so as not to soil his white shoes, Isaac picked his way through the market, crossed the street and reached his mother's home. The red-brick building, one of the many semi-detached houses in the African township, crouched over the pavement.

'Morning my son. I see you've bought another hat,' said Shoko, M'kama's second wife, as Isaac entered the kitchen, 'New shoes as well. What a lot of money you waste on clothing. I heard news on the radio about the strikes. Did you organise them?'

Shoko sat by a table in the open doorway. Her thick legs were warming in an oblong patch of sunlight. She watched the activities in the marketplace and heard fragments of gossip from the street. Isaac pulled out a chair and sat opposite her.

'Stop your chattering, Mother, and pour me some tea. Why don't you use china crockery? The peasants use these gaudy enamel things,' he said taking a mug of tea that she poured from a bright blue teapot.

'Did you plan the strikes?' Shoko repeated.

'Most of them. Now I need cash for rallies and protest marches. Will you give me the money?'

Shoko laughed. 'Why do you need money for that?'

'For renting venues and transporting the people.'

'The people won't bother attending. You heard the old hag a moment ago, she thinks you're stealing from her.'

'Others are stealing more. They're taking the wealth from the ground, farming the best lands. She will be well rewarded when we have our independence.'

'She won't listen to you.'

'Oh yes she will when she's promised a shop on Main Street and a big house in the suburbs. I must get the masses to the meetings where I will persuade them to unite in our struggle for our independence. Freedom and wealth that's what we want.'

'You mean, what *you want*.'

68

Shoko had petted and spoiled Isaac since childhood. He had inherited her features, a straight sharp nose and light brown complexion and her tall stature. Years ago in the early thirties a missionary visited Isaac's village. The boy proudly stepped from his hut wearing a handsome civet pelt across his shoulders. He greeted the distinguished visitor with poise and elegance.

'Your son is an exceptional lad, different from other boys of the tribe,' the missionary told the mother. He sniffed and stepped from the boy. The civet pelt was still fresh and not yet properly cured. 'I can see he is intelligent. One day he will lead the people. Allow him to attend school at the mission. We will name him Isaac.'

The missionary noticed a young woman sulking nearby. How unfortunate for that girl to be afflicted with a squint, thought the missionary. Her brother gets all the attention, no wonder she looks so bitter. There is more than one way to be lame.

'Name your daughter Gladys, it'll suit her,' suggested the missionary. 'When she is older, send her to the city, where there is an opportunity for her to earn a living.'

The mother gave a fleeting glance at her daughter. 'Yes, I will take her.' Going to her son, she touched his arm. 'Work hard and listen to the preacher for he has much to teach you.'

'Yes mother,' answered the boy impatiently. His mother couldn't imagine how far or fast Isaac wanted to get away from the village.

Obeying his mother's orders, he worked diligently and listened carefully.

'Thanks to the Lord,' prayed the preacher. 'I have found a true convert.'

Five years later Isaac passed his school examinations and took his place in modern society. His career began as a postal clerk. Practising diplomacy and working hard, he rose to a senior position. Shoko was proud of her son's achievement.

'Have you any new money-making projects?' asked Isaac.

'See that small brick building by the bus stop.'

69

'You mean the ticket office?'

'Yes, I'm in charge now. The Transport Company asked me to be their agent.'

'What do you do as an agent?'

'Sell bus tickets and keep the place clean. They pay me well.'

Isaac respected Shoko for her business acumen and intelligence. She had become wealthy since she and Gladys arrived in the city years ago. Shoko dabbled shrewdly in several enterprises, some of them shady deals and others were legitimate enterprises. She traded in various commodities, buying at low prices and making high profits. For a fee she aided many young girls in their time of trouble. Some merchants respected her for judgement and others admired her for her full figure.

'I want the wealthy settlers to join my Party. They'll give me more credibility,' said Isaac. 'There must be a way to encourage them.'

'Have you seen the art gallery on Main Street?'

'No. What gossip have you heard and what has it got to do with my problem?'

'This gallery is owned by a handsome woman, Mrs Marion Russell. She is new in town and is sympathetic to the plight of the peasants. She left her country in a hurry – marriage problems – arrived here and started this art business. It won't be a paying enterprise, too many white folk leaving. You should get to know her.'

'The time is not ripe for us to consort with the whites. I can't afford scandal.'

'Times have changed. We have become more tolerant to other races.'

'Maybe,' said Isaac, 'but I don't see how one white woman could help my Party.'

Shoko meditated as she absently watched the bustle in the marketplace. Squatting in the warmth of the morning sun, groups of native men chattered in melodious voices. Bare-arsed infants sat on yellow pumpkins under the tables. Water dripped from open taps to form muddy patches between the stalls. Bitches in whelp snarled at each other over rubbish bins. A youth screamed and pelted a cur with sharp rocks as it lifted its leg over a stack of cabbages. Tethered goats bleated. Roosters crowed from wicker baskets and ducks quacked.

'Marion Russell isn't important at the moment. Don't forget what I have told you,' said Shoko finally.

Isaac shrugged and asked. 'Where's Gladys?'

'Over there, across the street. Call her.'

Isaac went to the door and shouted to his sister across the street. She strolled over to the house and stood at his side.

'What do you want?'

'Are you still working for that wealthy family?'

'Auston-Jones, yes. When we first came here we stopped on the path and watched him dancing at his wedding feast.'

'That was almost nine years ago,' said Shoko. 'I remember how silly they all looked, all dressed up and dancing in the hot sun.'

'He has two sons now,' said Gladys. 'I'm a nanny to his second son, Jack. What do you want to know about Mr Auston-Jones?'

'What's he like and what does he do?'

'He's okay, he pays me well.' Gladys squinted at her brother. 'I think he oversees his estate and stables and paints a lot of pictures.'

'What kind of pictures?'

'Animals that are so alive they almost jump out of the painting. He paints trees. Trees that seem to grow every day. Why do you want to know?'

'I need his support. How can I meet him?' said Isaac and not waiting for an answer, he set his hat at a stylish angle and walked away.

Gladys called after him. 'I've quarters behind the house. Come and see me, maybe you'll meet the master. It's his eldest son's eighth birthday next month . . .'

71

Chapter 8

The following morning William stretched and pulled away as he became conscious of Hattie's breath on the nape of his neck. She lay cuddled with her knee pressed into the small of his back, and her warm feet curled under his tail. He turned over, allowing her to wriggle her shoulder into his armpit and opened her legs over his thighs. Twenty minutes later he lay above her and caressed her.

Footsteps approached the bedroom then there came a feathery bump on the carpet.

'I'll call him in,' suggested Hattie. 'He is at the door with his pillow.'

'What with me like this! My bare ass stuck up in the air.' William exclaimed before adding quietly. 'Give me a few more moments.'

Hattie held him close and waited. A spasm rippled through his body, as if a puppeteer jerked his bones and sinews into working order.

With a contented sigh William withdrew from her and swung his legs onto the floor. Groping under the bedclothes, he finally found his shorts and drew them on.

'Really William you're incorrigible. Patting yourself like that. One would think you've just completed a marathon.' She smiled and shook her head. He winked back at her.

The bedside radio clicked on, '. . . morning news. Wild-cat strikes across . . .' William grimaced and turned the radio off. He reached for Hattie's silk gown and wrapped it about her shoulders and remarked, 'Tyl is up before the damn bird who is after the worm.'

'Don't call our son, Tyl. I named him Liam because after all, he is part of you,' said Hattie. 'I'm sure a sorceress bewitched his laces. I tie them a dozen times a day and they still come undone.'

All who spoke to Liam prefixed their words with, 'Tie your laces.' William nicknamed the boy 'Tyl'.

'He's the image of my father, with the same deep-set eyes and high forehead. Like him, the boy is insane with bloody horses.' William said. 'He's eight years old today. Where have the years gone?' He pressed Hattie's thigh fondly and went back to his side of the bed. 'Come in Liam.'

The door handle turned and the door creaked open. A pillow was tossed into the room followed by a tall thin boy. His facial features, front teeth and nose appeared far too large for the small face.

'Why doesn't that child grow in proportion?' William frequently asked Hattie. 'First his limbs were too long for his body, now he's all teeth.'

'You probably were the same, all eyes, hands and feet.'

The tails of Liam's faded, check shirt hung out of his khaki shorts. The laces of his old sneakers trailed behind him.

Liam ran into his father's open arms and kissed his cheek. He then scrambled on his stomach over the bed, skinny legs raised, so not to soil the bedding. He cuddled into his mother's shoulder, breathing deeply. William watched. The boy always leaves the sweetest of his dessert until last.

Hattie kissed Liam's forehead and from under the pillow she drew a gaily wrapped parcel. 'Happy birthday, Liam.'

Ripping off the paper, Liam held up a book and said. 'Ah! Horses. Look, she is a beauty. Thanks Mom.' He immediately became absorbed in the illustrations.

'Open the curtains, Liam,' William ordered. The boy ignored the order.

'Liam!' William's sharp tone of voice brought the boy back to reality. 'Open the curtains.'

Liam slipped off the bed and padded over to the window.

74

He struggled with the brocade curtains, now slightly faded. After tugging, while his parents just sat watching, he managed to draw one back. He began to pull at the second. Below the window, the yard reached to the base of Pioneer Hill. To Liam's left, the jacaranda blossomed beyond the old bricked-up boiler. Across the yard Gladys rocked baby Jack in his blue stroller. Her red headscarf contrasted with her brown face and white uniform. She stood staring across at the house. Liam wondered what she could see.

He went closer to the window and stood on tiptoe. Peering down, he refused to believe his eyes, he blinked and looked again. Yes it was true! He did see a pony, shaking its bridle, impatient for the young rider. The stable boy holding the reins waved and pointed to the red bow attached to the saddle. Liam turned from the window and rushed into his father's arms. 'Thank you, Daddy. Oh! Thank you.' After a quick nuzzle against his mother's breasts, Liam ran from the room.

'Its name is Frith,' William shouted after Liam.

Together Hattie and William stood by the window. She felt William's strong body press against her as they watched Liam throw his arms about the pony's neck and kiss its cheek.

'My God, he did that to me. Does he think I'm a bloody horse?' said William. 'He's the fourth generation of crazy horse lovers. That child was born to ride. Bet his grandfather has a silly grin on his face.'

'Really my darling, you do have a weird imagination. Tell me, have we done the right thing? Has Liam enough strength to control that pony? It looks very strong to me.'

'It is. That's why I called it Frith after my father's ox that pulled his wagon. Besides, would anything less satisfy Liam? He's reckless, but we must let him follow his dreams. My father in his own selfish way protected me and denied me childish dreams. I spent my early years not knowing which way to go and became lost.' William stared down, not registering the scene below.

'Are you still lost?' Hattie asked quietly.

75

Sadly, he smiled. 'A little. With you beside me, Hatts, I'll find my way one day.'

'Search for your beautiful model, achieve your ambition, and become a renowned artist. I want you to do that. Promise me.'

'Maybe.' He turned from the window and looked at her. 'I worry about Liam too. Don't worry, my dear, after breakfast, I'll have a serious talk with him. God help him if I catch him disobeying me.'

Together the parents watched the stable boy hand Liam a riding hat and leg him up into the saddle. Liam took up the reins and urged the pony to canter from the yard.

William dropped his hand and pressed Hattie's inner thigh. He lifted his eyebrows suggestively and nodded at the bed.

'No. You've had enough – it's not your birthday. There's Gladys bringing Jack in for his nap. I must see to him in a moment.' Hattie began stripping the bed.

'Isn't Jack too big for a nanny?'

'She only minds him. You know how he wanders away.'

'Can you trust that woman? Why has she such a resentful attitude? We treat her well enough. Maybe it's her squint, she has the evil eye.'

'Nonsense, we should feel sorry for her. With her affliction she'll never marry. Besides I can understand her dialect.'

'Well, she'll never be a lady of the night. One never knows who she's looking at. That handsome fellow that visited her, who is he? He seems to hang around the place a lot. I wonder what he wants?'

'He's her brother, Isaac.'

'Isaac! Gladys! Who named them?'

'When they were children, a missionary came to their village and named them.'

'He chose a right name for her. I think the name Gladys means "lame". She looks like a lame duck, the way she waddles. Please be careful; I don't trust her.'

'Shame on you William! You must be more tolerant because she had a bad start in life. Isaac is extremely clever and high up in government circles.'

76

'Poor Gladys, she is left with the peasants. Really Hattie you do allow odd ones into the house.'

'Away with you and paint me another picture,' said Hattie.

'You have too many pictures. It's time they were sold.'

'Not until you are a famous painter, besides they're personal, like love letters.'

William picked up Liam's pillow and threw it at her. She ducked and made for the door before he had another idea.

Hattie smiled her thanks when William held the chair for her at the breakfast table. Before he went back to his chair, he fingered the silk scarf about her hair. The colour matched her eyes.

'Did you get all the news?' she asked.

'Yes. Strikes across the country. The workers are demanding higher wages, more schools and hospitals. How can we meet all their demands? How can a few Europeans support so many?' he said taking his plate from her. 'We must take more security precautions, lock the doors at night. I'll repair the broken fence, discourage Africans from coming through the property. Where are the children?'

'Jack's taking a nap. Liam is waiting for you. I'll call him.'

Liam waited by his father's side, his elbow on the table his feet crossed at the ankles. Someone had tried to tie his shoe laces. 'Dad, you wanted to see me.'

'Yes.' William continued to read the morning paper.

Scuffling his feet, Liam looked down. William folded the paper slowly, deliberated. For Hattie's peace of mind, Liam must be safeguarded; but how? How could he explain to a small boy that each of us are responsible for what we love and those who love us? William's thoughts reached into his past, searching for an answer. Through obedience, and fear of the unknown consequences if he had disobeyed, he had endured. This was the only way he knew how to caution his son. Demand obedience and instil fear.

'Look at me, boy.' William commanded.

Astonished at his father's harsh voice, Liam cringed. The expression in William's eyes, the same as rusted tacks, ripped

77

through Liam. William's facial muscles like knotted cords, pulled the lips into thin cruel line. Liam saw the hands poised on the table. The strong fingers, curled into the palms ready to squeeze the breath from him. Who was this frightful stranger? His father!

'Listen very carefully.' The words fell like splintered glass. 'You will obey every detail of my instructions. They concern your safety and responsibility.'

Apprehension made Liam tremble, he swallowed hard. His father's precise instructions began. Stay within the estate's boundaries. Listen and follow his instructor orders to the letter. There will be no insolence, cheek or giving orders to the stable hands. The pony was Liam's responsibility: feeding, grooming and mucking out its stall. Other orders followed.

William finally said, 'You do understand my commands?'

Liam whispered. 'Yes.'

'You will obey them. Go now.'

Liam backed away to the door and scuttled down the passage slamming the screen door behind him.

After pouring a third cup of tea, William followed his son onto the veranda. The family spent most of their time on the porch. It caught the winter sun in the mornings and in summer it held the cool breeze.

He sat on a large toy-box and glanced at the children's breakfast dishes that cluttered their table. A bright cover had replaced Grandmother's patchwork quilt on the divan. Sipping his tea, he studied the almost finished painting and thought, I wonder where Hattie will hang this one. His third masterpiece hung in the dining-room, it had replaced the photograph of the grim-looking father.

The morning wore on. William painted the sap of sunshine here, a happy shadow there. He looked up again at his subject – his brows knitted.

'Well I am b . . .' He dropped his brush, walked to the end of the veranda and peered at the jacaranda tree. Going back to the screen door, he shouted down the passage. 'Hattie, come here a sec.'

Hattie straightened the small watercolour hanging in the passage as she answered. 'In a minute, Jack's awake.'

After checking with her household staff in the kitchen, she entered the day nursery, a narrow room at the end of the passage and tucked under the stairs.

'Good morning, my baby,' said Hattie. 'Did your father wake you up? I wonder what's agitating him. Probably a beetle or worm has invaded his space. It's about time he found his beautiful model.'

This was mother and son's special time together and nothing hurried them. William often feigned jealousy, and complained. 'You converse more to that child than to me.'

Hattie placed her forearms on the cot and smiled down at the child. 'You know, I don't know whom you look like. Your hair is the same as your father's, the dark brown of roan antelope. It's really sexy. He likes me to do this.' Hattie ran her fingers through Jack's curls. He gurgled in response. 'Your Dad insists your eyes are like mine. Lilac, he says they are.'

Jack reached for the slats and pulled himself upright. Hattie went on chatting to him. 'There is something else that I'll tell you. He has dark hair in other places; very, very sexy indeed.' Hattie allowed a naughty smile. 'Here is another secret.' She took the small hand through the slats and placed it on her stomach. 'Feel there. Soon you'll have a baby brother or sister. Don't tell Daddy now. He fusses too much.'

Jack pouted his lips and held out his arms.

'Let me dress you, then we'll go to him. He's painting a hippopotamus. Can you say that long word?'

The child drew his fair brows together, and tried to frown. A bubble appeared on his soft lips. Sucking it in and forming his lips into a circle, he said, 'ot.'

'Well done, an otomus,' she encouraged him. 'Your father says you're too old for a nanny. He is right because you are almost four years old.'

'ainting,' said Jack pointing to a large picture.

'Yes, there's an owl and there's the moon and see down

79

here some fireflies.' A memory made her smile. 'One day Daddy will sneak in here and add a frog in this corner.'

The picture was her favourite. It was the first of William's masterpieces. Each creature accurately portrayed, true to colour and condition.

'Hattie,' William called again.

'Coming.'

Jack leaned out of her arms.

'What do you want, Jack?'

'Aggerty.'

'Of course, you want Our Haggerty.' Hattie bent her knees and picked up a teddy bear from the cot.

'I remember when Uncle Seth bought this for Liam. It was a long time ago.'

'This is specially for you, a Haggerty bear. All the children like these bears,' Seth had told the infant Liam. Liam focused his eyes on the toy and screamed. William, by the doorway, bent double and howled with laughter. Wiping tears from his eyes, he eventually spluttered:

'Frankly I agree with Liam. That is a hideous stuffed toy. I never saw anything so bloody appalling, a teddy bear dressed in a white petticoat and a green checked apron.'

'William! Don't swear, not in front of the child,' exclaimed Hattie as she came into the nursery.

Seth looked hurt. 'Rubbish!' he said, 'That's what Haggerty bears wear. I'm sure Liam will like it. Maybe he's yelling because of colic or is in pain.'

'Don't be ridiculous, it frightened the hell out of the child.' William laughed.

The stuffed toy sat neglected in the cupboard for years. One day Hattie offered it to baby Jack. It was love at first sight. He claimed the bear.

Liam once demanded the toy. 'It's my Haggerty,' he pulled it away. Jack screamed and kicked.

'It's mine,' insisted Liam teasing his little brother.

'Let's call it Our Haggerty,' suggested Hattie. The name stuck.

Hattie, holding Jack in her arms, smoothed the white petti-

80

coat on the bear. 'What have we got in Our Haggerty's pocket? Your childish treasures?'

Hattie never realised that one day the pocket would hold the family's fortune.

Liam came into the room and said, 'Father is calling you. He said to come quickly.'

'Thank you, sweetheart. We're coming.' Hattie opened the pocket. 'A button, some string. What beautiful treasures. One day I'll show you my treasure. It's in the wardrobe, in a small blue box. What else have you ... a rock? Oh no young man! Don't you start prospecting for gold at this age. You're not to be like your grandfather Carver. He went crazy with the gold fever.'

With those words she swept out the room holding Jack close to her heart. On the veranda she said,

'You wanted me, what's wrong?'

William pointed to the jacaranda tree. Its blossoms had formed a purple carpet at the base of the tree.

'Look,' exclaimed William.

'Where?'

'Under the jacaranda.'

With her hand Hattie shaded her eyes from the sunlight.

'Dear Heavens! What is that and where did it come from?' she cried.

Chapter 9

'Is it a person?' Hattie asked as she peered from the veranda. 'Or has someone left a bundle of rags under the tree?'

'It's a man; he just appeared out of thin air,' answered William.

The man, in tattered clothes and mud-caked feet that bled from small wounds, lay slumped against the trunk of the tree. Hunger and exhaustion had paled his dark complexion.

'That poor sick man, however did he get there?' said Hattie as she put Jack down. 'Off you go and play, my child.'

'I told you, he appeared out of thin air,' William said.

Avoiding the rickety step, Hattie ran to the jacaranda tree and crouched beside the man. The African lifted his head and partially opened his fiery red eyes as she touched his forehead. William strode up with his hands in his pockets. He leaned back placing the sole of his shoe against the trunk.

Hattie raised her head and spoke to him. 'This unfortunate soul,' she said, 'has a raging temperature. See the skin, how taut it is across his cheekbones.'

'Hm, wonder where he comes from?'

'He's from the area where Seth farms. Some of his workers have the same markings on their temples. What are we going to do, we can't leave him here. Let's get him to the hospital.'

'No. It's too dangerous to move him. He's suffering from an acute dose of malaria. I can tell by the trembling. The shivers are starting, that's the first symptom; the chills will follow.'

William could not forget the torments of malaria. How his body had felt on fire. He recalled the perspiration oozing from every pore and drenching the bedclothes. The cold and the shivers followed. Hours after uncontrollable shivering, came the fatigue and utter weakness.

'Yes,' William concluded. 'He has the fever and besides, the poor chap is close to starvation and he's extremely weak.'

A worried frown deepened in Hattie's forehead. 'What'll happen if we move him? I don't know much about malaria.'

'Liver, spleen and kidneys might disintegrate. The disease develops into blackwater fever.'

Hattie nodded. 'Now I remember. That is when the urine turns black or dark red.'

'Stay here with him.' William pushed himself away from the tree. 'I'll get the Mepacrine, it's the new improved prophylactic for the treatment of malaria.'

'Can't we take him into the servants' quarters, for protection from the heat?'

'With a tin roof over a square room, he'll think he's in Hell,' William answered and went to the house. 'I'll get the workers to stack some grass above his head. That'll make him feel at home.'

'Don't be so callous,' Hattie shouted back. William waved a hand in reply.

When Hattie soothed the fevered brow again with a cool hand, the patient focused his eyes and stared at her.

'Good day, my friend, I thank you for coming to see us. Please stay for as long as you wish. What is your name?' she greeted him in a dialect she had learnt in her childhood.

The man mumbled, through painful dried cracked lips. 'Jour . . .'

'It sounds like Job, maybe the prophet himself,' said William returning with tablets and a mug of water.

'Job wasn't a prophet. No, it's an unusual name, but it doesn't matter. Let's wait until he has improved.'

William, dubious at the chances of the man's recovery, raised his eyebrows. 'Don't get your hopes up. This man is

84

seriously ill. We'll do what we can, give him plenty of liquids and a course of the tablets. I don't think he'll survive.'

Hattie put the tablets in the man's mouth and let him drink from the mug. 'This medicine will make the heat in your head go way.' She twisted around to see Liam cantering up on Frith. He reined in and looked down at the sick man.

'What is his name?' he asked.

'He muttered something like Ju . . . Jourbor,' answered Hattie.

'I saw him at the market. Remember Mama when we took Uncle Seth's parcel to the bus depot.'

'Hattie!' shouted William throwing up his hands, his eyes becoming pinpoints. The red flushes of anger rose from his neck to his face. 'For God's sake, what were you doing there alone. I've told you often enough. It's dangerous. A white woman on her own is asking for trouble.'

'I wanted to send Seth a birthday gift. Oparee, the bus driver, said he would drop it at The Junction. That's where Seth collects his mail.'

'I am not interested . . .' William began hotly but Liam interrupted.

'While you were talking to the bus driver, I saw this man sitting close by. He kept looking at your legs.'

Placated by Liam's remark, William said, 'Well, I must say the fellow has good taste and some class.'

'Go on with you . . . you're incorrigible,' chortled Hattie.

For two days and two nights William and Hattie attended to sick Jourbor. Late into the third night they sat, waiting. The naked bulb suspended low from the tree swayed slowly, distorting a circle of dull light.

'Surely he can't hang on much longer, he's been so ill for these past three days,' Hattie sobbed. 'His condition is deteriorating.'

'Hold on, darling, the fever is reaching a climax. We'll persevere,' encouraged William as he sponged the African's perspiring body. He used a towel soaked in vinegar – it cooled the body and lowered the temperature. The six-hour

85

cycle of the fever had begun again. Two hours of uncontrollable shivering followed by two hours of raging temperatures, and then came chills and the perspiring. Hattie placed two tablets in Jourbor's mouth and held cold water to his lips.

'This white man's medicine won't make your ears sing like swarming bees. It's not like the grounded pods that come from the muora tree. Those pods taste bitter and they make the noise of the cricket in your head.'

'Tell him that the tablets will chase the devils out of his black soul.'

'You've a macabre sense of humour. I don't understand you. One moment you are compassionate, the next, so facetious,' Hattie chided.

'It helps to face the horrors of death.'

Hattie went into his arms and sobbed. 'Oh William, William. Please don't let him die.'

'Hush, my sweetheart, there is nothing more we can do. Come you must get some rest. I'll check on him through the night.'

William led Hattie up the veranda steps and into the house, as rain clouds rolled down from the north-west and shadows vanished in the blackness. Above Jourbor's makeshift shelter the naked bulb swung, confusing his dreams in an uneasy sleep. He moaned and twisted, his mind rambling. Pictures, framed in hazy mists advanced and receded. Garbled noises reached crescendos then diminished to eerie whispers.

In visions he saw the grey lourie, and heard its call, 'goway, go-way-way'. The call resounded through black heavy clouds and a confusion of glowing embers. He looked up and shuddered at a face in the tree. Two round yellow eyes glowed. Were they, the large eyes of the tree god? She hung there, as if waiting for his soul.

Morning brought the worst spectacle of all. It began the moment the owl took flight as the dawn broke, and Jourbor's fever reached new heights. A cacophony of barking dogs began. The noise conjured a fantasy of loathsome creatures protecting their own. Then the boy who couldn't use his legs appeared. This thin youth rode around the garden on a

86

strange contraption. At times he rode on the back of the wild animal. With the clatter of receding hooves Jourbor was sure he heard his mother's voice.

'No Jourbor. No, I'm sure the eagle didn't take your prayer to the gods.'

'It's not on the river bank.' Jourbor held out his hand to his mother. Her image diffused in the mist, his memory receding. Blackness followed until a pale light glowed again.

'Maybe the impala trampled it into the mud when they came down to drink.' Leena's voice came from afar. 'I saw their flashing white tails when I went for water.'

'No . . . no . . .' Jourbor heard himself cry. He had not forgotten the storyteller's advice. 'Kangera, kangera. Look. around you and observe.'

'Yes Mother, I took the hunter's advice. I studied the wood of the trees. Look at the smooth grain in this.' In his delirium Jourbor held up a carved lion. 'It makes fine lines for the lion's mane.'

Jourbor had shown his mother the different coloured clay he'd used for the bowls and various articles. Leena just nodded and shrugged. Why does he just sit by the fire carving? He isn't like other boys hunting and showing their strength at wrestling games. Soon he must take a wife.

Summer cooled into autumn then came a mild winter. With the coming of spring, villagers from distant villages passed Leena's small settlement, carrying bundles of crafts and produce. They were on their way to sell these goods at a trading store in the south. Some people passed, never to return. Those who did come back wore new clothes and carried bags of ground corn and neatly wrapped parcels. Many had factory-made cigarettes hanging from their mouths.

'Have you seen any crazy white gods?' Jourbor asked the next traveller, who was dressed in smart clothes and shiny shoes.

The traveller put down his bundle of goods and bellowed with laughter. 'White gods! You mean the white men, they're not gods. You're right though, they're mad and very peculiar.'

87

He opened his bundle. 'Look at these rocks. See all those glittering yellow spots. The man with red hair on his chin will pay me if I tell him where I found these. He grows corn, a half-day's walk from here. Have you not seen him?'

Leena remained quiet. The stream close by was scattered with rocks with yellow spots. She wanted no white man, crazy or not, to invade her settlement.

The next woman who came by Leena asked, 'Where is this trading store? Some people call it The Junction.'

'It's a four-day walk, that way.' The visitor described the trading store, the trader and the shady tree where people exchange news.

'Mother,' said Jourbor one day. 'I notice you always look at the women's head-dresses. Would you like one?'

'No. They're too rough and are not like the colour in the rainbow.'

Jourbor shook his head at Leena's cryptic remark. Women were strange.

When mothers and their teenage daughters passed by, Leena invited them to the hearth. She fed them choice rodents and well-cooked corn. They all thanked her politely but ignored her son. Jourbor sat by silently modelling clay or carving bowls.

To one regular visitor Leena confided, 'Could my son trade his handicraft for a wife at The Junction?' she asked.

The visitor politely hid her smile. 'Oh! Yes. A man can trade a wife for one night or two, maybe for longer.'

While the rain poured down during the summer, Leena deliberated. By autumn she had reached a decision. Gathering the rushes from the river, she wove them into two large baskets. One calm evening, as they sat by the fire, Leena spoke to Jourbor.

'I've packed your bowls and carvings in these baskets. Tomorrow as the sun rises you must set off for The Junction. Remember when the egrets fly in formation to their feeding grounds, keep them over your right shoulder. At noon you must rest. When your shadow lengthens be sure the sun is

88

over your left shoulder and continue your journey. Walk for four days then you'll reach The Junction.

'There you will trade your goods for a wife. Take care whom you choose. She must be able to skin rodents quickly and cleanly. Make sure she knows how to grind the corn, not too small nor leave the kernels too big. Look at her hips. Wide hips will show she can produce many children.'

So on a fresh morning Jourbor turned away from his patch. He started off into the twentieth century to trade his handicraft for a productive wife.

'I'm sorry,' said the trader, 'there is no sale for your work here. There is no market now for bowls and carvings. Go to the city, there you might find a wife.'

'How do I get there?'

'By bus. It'll be here soon.' Soon, could mean within hours or maybe a day.

Jourbor sat and slept under the tree while he waited. He listened to the talk about him. He waited. Two days later the bus rattled up and braked in front of the store.

'Will you take me to the city?' Jourbor asked the bus driver.

Oparee grinned, displaying his beautiful white teeth. 'Yes, I'll take you. The city is far from here, it's a six-hour journey.'

Jourbur scratched his head. 'Six hours! That is nearby. It took me four days to get here.'

'Well, you see the bus travels at thirty miles . . . Oh never mind, you won't understand. Get in and I'll drop you off at the market.'

Jourbor sat very upright in his seat, looking neither left nor right. It's better not to look if you don't understand your surroundings. He had to keep awake, so not to miss the city.

Six hours later the driver braked at the bus depot.

'Go to that red-brick room, that's the bus depot,' he said to Jourbor. 'Shoko, a handsome woman, will help you. She'll understand your dialect, and show you where to sell your craft. Her son is very clever. He went to school.'

Jourbor went into the bus depot. He didn't feel very comfortable under the tin roof. Shoko waddled in, lifted part

89

of the counter and passed through. Facing him from the other side, she recognised the marking on his temple, a clan she disliked. Her husband, M'kama, visited these valley people. He said they were kind and generous. She thought them repulsive, with their short bodies and thick shoulders. Also, they were lazy and full of diseases from the river.

'Well, what do you want?' she asked Jourbor.

He greeted her politely and asked where he could sell his craft. Also, he'd like to buy a wife.

Shoko hooted with laughter as she took the superbly carved models from him. Inspecting the form of a deer, she licked her lips with greed.

'Here, I'll save you the trouble, I'll buy these.' Shoko gave him a few coins. 'That is all it's worth.' With a chubby hand she waved him away. Bewildered and lost, Jourbor looked at the money. These coins meant nothing to him; he came for a wife not bits of metal!

Jourbor left the hot tin-roof room and wandered about. He disliked what he saw. There were too many people in one place, all talking and making an awful noise. Half-naked children with mucous oozing from their nostrils sat listlessly in the heat. Flies gathered over rotting fruit and the smelly wild herbs that dried in the sun. Women shrieked at youths who rudely pushed their way through the stalls. From the street came the noise of cars revving and blaring horns.

Jourbor returned to the bus depot; he sat on a wooden crate waiting and wanting to go home. His head hurt and his throat burned. Maybe Oparee, the bus driver, would come to take him away from this dreadful place. Eventually, he dozed off, his arms and head on his knees.

'Please give this parcel to the bus driver. He will leave it at The Junction.' These words filtered into Jourbor's dazed mind.

He lifted his head and looked into the bus depot. He saw a woman leaning over the counter. Idly he glanced at the bare legs. Where had he seen a scar shaped like that? Yes, now he remembered, the little river god, she had a scar like that. Yes, yes, now he recalled the hunter with the leopard

90

skin draped from his shoulders and the long spear and a wooden shield. The brave hunter wanted to kill the little river god. Jourbor's recollections receded in his mind then became clear again. The blemish shaped like the drongo's long feathery tail. He lowered his aching head. The fever was on him again. Later, when he opened his eyes, the speaker had vanished. He had to find her again. Slowly rising, he staggered into the depot.

'Do you know that person?' he asked Shoko.

'Yes.'

'Do you know where that person lives?'

The woman pointed to the coins in his hand. He understood and gave them back to her.

'My daughter works for her. She will show you the way. Gladys!' A buxom young woman came from the rear of the room.

'It's time you were at work. Show this man the way to the big house.'

Gladys summed up Jourbor with a sneer. Ignoring his greetings, she turned and left him to follow. They walked through the market and past several trading stores. Finally they arrived at the edge of the town and Gladys took a well trodden path leading northwards. Jourbor, smelling the freshness of the country, was grateful to leave the dust and noise of the marketplace. He asked Gladys if this path led to his home, four days away. She pouted and ignored him. As she stepped over the broken fence, her white uniform stretched across her firm buttocks.

Jourbor twisted around when he heard the frightful clatter. A freakish animal with a small rider on its back charged at him. Its hooves pounded the dusty path and steam poured from large red nostrils. The man hesitated no longer and dived head first into the bushes. The rider galloped past, looking straight ahead. Jourbor remained motionless, until the noise faded. He emerged from his hiding place with twigs and dried leaves sticking to his hair. Gladys stood with one hand on her hip, the other pointing a finger at him. Her painted lips opened wide as she roared with laughter.

'You fool. Haven't you seen a horse before?'

She spun around and ran along the path. Her laughter, not unlike the screech of the grey lourie, faded in the distance.

With fire burning in his body and sweat running down his face, Jourbor staggered along the slight incline. Then he saw the ethereal colour, the seventh colour of the rainbow, the jacaranda in full bloom. He went forward.

'Hatts!' Jourbor heard a voice calling from across the garden before he fell unconscious under the tree.

During the following days Jourbor became aware of unusual sounds and weird shapes dissolving only to form again. There were times when a cool hand stroked his hot brow. Blankets warmed him when he shivered. Well after dawn on the third day he saw a fire burning brighter than the sunlight. It shone past the shadows of the tree. He held out his hands, his memory receding, and whispered: 'Mother, I'm coming. I'm coming home.'

Chapter 10

A rooster extended his neck, crowed twice then flapped his colourful feathered tail. The power struggle between night and day began. Shadows flickered from grey to light grey. Nocturnal animals slunk to their dens and scratched at their bedding before snuggling down. Day hunters opened an eye, stretched a paw or twitched a whisker. Hunger pains gnawed. Bees agitated over the unopened buds. A child's laughter rippled from the depth of the house. Night relented. Dawn glowed. Melodious greetings to the sun wafted from the valley and nearby a puppy yelped. The tree dropped its pod with a resounding plop. The new day began.

An hour later, William pulled his sweater over his head as he shouldered the screen door and strolled onto the veranda. Impassively he watched a robin brace its thin legs and tug at an earthworm. The worm wriggled frantically and slipped through the robin's beak. Twittering, the bird flew off.

'Stupid bloody bird,' William said aloud and shuffled to his easel to pick up his paint brush. He always felt a small victory when the worm won the tug-of-war.

Hattie came out and glanced across the garden.

'He's gone,' she said.

William added a stroke of colour, stepped back and mumbled. 'Relinquished his black soul to the devil?'

'No. I mean he has gone, physically. He's not there.'

'The ungrateful sod. He never said goodbye or thanks to you. Ah! Here comes our cowboy, on his bicycle.'

Liam braked and supported his foot on the bottom step.

'He hasn't gone. Look there, he is sitting by the boiler.'

'Well I'll be bug . . .' began William.

'William! Not in front of the child,' Hattie said.

'He's stoking the boiler,' Liam added.

William squinted through narrowed eyes at his work. 'Hm, proper Satan's little helper.'

'No wonder the kitchen water was so hot,' said Hattie, and tripped lightly down the steps.

'Don't let that creature into my house,' William called as he leered at her swaying hips under the floral skirt. It's not only the eyes that seduce a man, he thought.

Jourbor, kneeling in front of the boiler, blew up the embers. Carefully he placed chips of wood and built up the flames. He smiled at Hattie as she repeated the traditional welcome and added. 'The fever has passed, but you must still take the white man's medicine.'

He lowered his eyes. Should he tell her he knew she was the river god? No. He had better not, it might bring misfortune. Nor would he mention the elephants and the spider who protected her. Now it was up to him to guard her. By the boiler he would stay and watch over her.

So he did. Blending into the household, Jourbor's presence became accepted by the domestic staff. He held no threat to their positions. Gladys was the only person to resent him. Egged on by her mother's dislike for his tribe, she humiliated him at every opportunity. Jourbor vowed silently. His day of retribution would dawn.

From the boiler Jourbor became familiar with the family's activities. The thin boy, Liam, either cycled around the jacaranda or galloped his horse across the fields. A smaller child played in the sand-box or wandered off on his own. Gladys would appear as if from nowhere and trail after the boy and bring him back. The eccentric man wore threadbare jeans and a blue-green sweater when he painted. The sweater sagged below his waist and rode up his bony wrists. Darning wool of different hues gave the article a mottled appearance. Yet, at the end of the day, this untidy man dressed for dinner, tying his black tie with care.

94

'Why do you keep the fire burning?' Hattie asked Jourbor who stood at the kitchen door watching her bake bread. 'I don't need hot water all the time.'

He tried to tell her this was his purpose in life, to provide hot water for her rituals, for she washed her hands religiously before baking bread. Jourbor mumbled an explanation but Hattie found the words bewildering.

She nodded her head and said. 'Come, sit by the table. I'll show you how to bake bread.'

Jourbor watched carefully.

'Kangera, kangera. Observe,' the old hunter had tutored him.

Jourbor washed his hands thoroughly in hot water. He believed this was the religious path to the success of the bread baking. He noted the ingredients: flour, salt, milk and yeast and the kneading. Hattie saw the strength in his hands and invited him to knead the mixture. Then she showed him how to cover the dough and keep it warm. Jourbor never knew what caused the dough to rise. It must be Hattie's supernatural powers. Baking bread became Jourbor's passion. Every morning there were two fresh loaves cooling on the kitchen table.

So Jourbor spent his days in tranquillity. Except for William's outbursts of panic and cursing, which set Jack off into shrieks of laughter. Hattie usually muttered soothingly and without concern, 'Not in front of the children, dear,' or she might add, 'It's time you found your beautiful model.'

Tuesday. Yes, remembered Jourbor, it was on a Tuesday morning. The day began as usual until Hattie called from the bathroom.

'Liam tell your father a fuse has blown in the heater. There is no hot water.'

No hot water! Jourbor held his head in shame. What had he done wrong? Was not the fire burning as it should? Immediately, he began stoking up the boiler.

'William! William!' shouted Hattie sometime later, 'The outside wall, it's getting hot.'

Hearing her shout, William dropped his brushes and flung

himself down the passage into the kitchen and placed his hand on the wall. He became hysterical.

'The bloody boiler! It's going to blow up! Get the kids out of the house. Christ! What is that moron up to?'

'Hush, William not in front of the children.'

'Dad's flapping again,' remarked Liam as he and Jack watched their father slam out of the kitchen and leap down the two steps. His sweater sagged below his buttocks. Into the vegetable garden he dashed and grabbed the wheelbarrow. Mumbling as he dragged the squeaking wheelbarrow through the gooseberry patch, 'I must oil the bloody wheel.'

The squeaking reached an ear-splitting pitch as he ran across the yard. At the boiler, he shoved it against the brick-work and climbed on. Stretching his forearm he grabbed the rusted faucet. It wouldn't open. Sweating and cursing he added extra pressure. Steam blew high into the air. Horrified, Jourbor watched all the water he had heated billowing away. In fury, he stamped on the ground. All his efforts wasted, the hot water going cold.

'You, you son of a spotted hyena. You overgrown wild dog,' he screamed in his own lingo as he pulled William off the wheelbarrow.

'Murder him,' coached Gladys from the servants' quarters. 'I'll tell the police he was killing you.'

'Bite your tongue!' Jourbor yelled back. Grabbing William by the back of the neck, he frogmarched him into the first bathroom. Down went William's head into the bath as Jourbor turned the tap on. With his stubby finger, pink palms close to William's vision, he pointed to the trickle of cold water.

Bent like a hairpin over the bath, William managed to point to the ceiling. 'Let me up, idiot. The boiler outside doesn't heat the bathroom water. The electric heater is up there.' He waggled a finger.

'What is he pointing to the gods for?' wondered Jourbor. The man is a blathering blockhead. Hattie stood at the door pressing her arms against her stomach, unable to control her laughter.

96

'For Christ sake, explain to him, Hattie.' William kicked out. Jourbor dodged the onslaught.

Hattie brushed away the tears of laughter with the palm of her hand. 'He . . . he'll never understand.'

All William could see from his bent position was her abdomen. 'You're pregnant?' he shouted.

Jourbor released William and went out beating the air with his hands. 'The man's an idiot. He sleeps with her and doesn't know his wife is with child. White men! White men! They are all crazy.'

Jourbor had known the first time Hattie felt his brow that she was with child. Through her touch he had sensed the aura of motherhood.

Cape gooseberry jam! Jourbor licked his lips at the very thought of gooseberry jam. Jam making and baking bread justified his existence.

In the early mornings Hattie and Jourbor began the process of preserving the fruit. From the bedroom window, William looked down at them in the gooseberry patch. He watched Jourbor obsequiously offering a berry for her inspection. Jourbor, the self-appointed slave, would die for her and he wasn't the only one. Why did all men want to kneel at her feet? Was it her grace, her tenderness that touched them?

Together and silently Hattie and Jourbor prepared and preserved the fruit. Jourbor decided the recipe for Cape gooseberry jam originated from the gods. No man could contrive such a heavenly delicacy.

'I don't want any,' William shrieked when he saw the jar filled with gooseberry jam. 'It smells and tastes like stinkbugs.'

'More for us,' said Liam and licked at the traces of jam around his lips.

Silently, like a shadow, Jourbor slipped into the lives of the family. The place beside the boiler became his home. Contentedly, he dreamed and accepted what he did not understand. There were no greys in Jourbor's life. White was white and black was black. Day dawned after night. Death

97

came after life. The ways of other gods were no concern of his. He remained content as long as he could bake bread, preserve the gooseberries and keep the fire going.

Jourbor did only one personal task for William. While Hattie sat on the top step admiring the sunset and William lolled on the divan watching her, Jourbor quietly cleaned William's paint brushes.

Later, after supper when he served tea, he watched them play dominoes. At first he thought they were speaking with the gods until Liam showed him how to play. Why did Hattie and William play it with such intensity? Jourbor did not realise their stakes were high. The loser must provide the night's activity in the bedroom. If William lost, he used his artistry, if Hattie did, she used her imagination. Neither remembered who had lost when Jack was conceived.

Only once did Hattie have misgivings about Jourbor's presence in the house. She asked William while at the lunch table, 'Have you seen my silk headscarf? The one you gave me, the purple one?' she asked.

'Not purple, Hattie, there is a subtle difference in colours. It's lilac and I haven't seen it.'

'Mauve, purple or indigo, I can't find it, I left it in the kitchen.'

'No doubt that drifter you allowed into the house stole it. I warned you about bringing all sorts in.'

'Jourbor! Why would he steal that?'

'Who'd know that? We can't be too careful. Those days of trust have gone. People are hungry for independence.'

Hattie answered. 'Yes and so it must be, but why would he take it?'

'Probably to perform some black magic.'

'Oh William! You and your imagination!' Hattie laughed but silently she agreed. Why did Jourbor steal it? Why would he want it?

The birth of Hattie's child came unexpectedly early, the labour pains starting one Sunday morning. William saw her grimace while she rested on the couch. 'What's up, something wrong?'

'There's a queer feeling in my back. It's been there all day. Don't worry, it's two weeks before the baby is due. I want to walk down to the paddocks.'

'It's too far.'

'William, do stop fussing,' said Hattie irritably. 'I want to see Liam at the jumps.'

The afternoon held the spring's warmth as Hattie and William returned from the stables.

'You look tired, my dear,' William said.

'Yes,' she admitted. 'I have a back pain. I'll rest when we get home.'

Two hours later Hattie called, 'William, William.'

He closed his book and went into the bedroom. 'What is it?'

'I think the baby's coming.'

'It's not due for two weeks.'

'The baby doesn't know that,' said Hattie. The pain increased. 'Get the doctor.'

William ran to the wall phone in the passage and rang the hospital. 'Come on. Come on, answer, will you.' He slammed the wall with his palm, shaking the small watercolour that hung nearby.

The sister-in-charge answered. 'General Hospital . . .'

'Auston-Jones here. Get Dr Thomas, hurry the baby is coming,' yelled William.

'Mr Auston-Jones your wife's doctor is away this week-end,' answered the nurse with composure.

'For Christ sakes! Get another doctor out here then.'

The calm voice ignored William's oaths. 'Doctor Hasling is visiting your neighbours. He has only just arrived, comes from . . .'

'I don't care if he dropped from Heaven and is visiting Hell, get him here.' William slammed down the phone and rushed back to Hattie.

'A doctor will be here shortly. Maybe it's a false alarm.'

'Make some tea in the blue teapot then call Liam. I want you all to be together. There is hot water for tea . . .'

Jourbor pattered down the passage just in time to hear

99

'hot water'. Now was the time he could serve his mistress. She needed hot water and no one would stop him this time. He quietly left the passage.

William bellowed from the veranda. 'Liam. Liam.' The reply came faintly from the paddocks. 'Coming Dad.'

Liam turned his pony and galloped up to the house. He threw the reins over the hitching post and grabbed his cycle. Lifting it onto the veranda, he opened the screen door. Jack sat against the day nursery door at the end of the passage. It was a good advantage point. From there he could see down the second passage and up the stairs leading to the landing. If he stretched his neck, he could see the yard through the narrow window.

'Where's Dad?' asked Liam.

Jack pointed up the stairs. 'Doctor is coming. Dad's flapping,' Jack answered and looked out the window. 'Jourbor is feeding the fire.'

Liam eyed the long passage. It was the perfect surface to try a stunt on his cycle. For weeks he practised standing on the crossbar, but the ground outside was too uneven. If he could get enough speed down the passage, he might do it. He let the screen door bang as he pushed his cycle into the passage. Giving a mighty shove, he jumped on the saddle. Half way down the passage, Liam gained his balance on the crossbar.

At that moment William came scooting out the bedroom and down the stairs. Jack saw his father's sneakers on the last step. The boy drew up his legs and squashed himself as close as possible in the corner.

'Sorry Jack. The doctor's at the door,' shouted William and flattened himself against the wall as the trick cyclist shot passed.

'Well done, my boy,' commented William and ran to the front door.

Although Doctor Hasling had difficulty acclimatising himself to the altitude and the heat, he was grateful to Rona Bentwood. Through her goodwill and her assortment of relatives, he obtained the position as a medical assistant at the

100

hospital. Here he could study tropical diseases. Unfortunately, he did not understand the colonists. They worked hard but he never saw them at it. Many wealthy people were eccentric. They wore their old shabby clothes and isolated themselves in their palatial homes.

'Don't rush. The baby isn't due for a good two weeks,' the sister-in-charge advised over the phone. 'Ask your friends to direct you to the patient's home.'

Doctor Hasling drove sedately along the tree-lined road, around the circular driveway and braked at the wide porch. Frith, the pony on the other side of the hedge, nibbled at the flowers. The animal gave a brief glance at the new arrival then continued to cull the plants. The doctor shivered and left the car. With his white cuffs showing the regulated two inches at his wrists and the tweed jacket pulled straight, he climbed the polished steps. Before ringing the bell, he wiped his brow.

At that moment the door was opened. A bony hand flapping from a skinny wrist grabbed the doctor by the shirt front. A tall man pulled him down the passage. They passed the first lounge and the second. Through the dining-room door he caught a glimpse of a thin child cycling around a long table, the Persian rugs tossed aside.

A small boy sat huddled near the stairs.

'Sorry Jack,' said the man as he pulled the astounded doctor up the stairs. In a large bedroom a pale woman lay sweating in labour. She raised her head and pointed out of the window.

'Jourbor's at the fire,' she panted.

'Oh Christ! Not again,' exclaimed the man and rushed out of the bedroom and down the passage.

Jack pulled back his feet again as his father's sneakers flapped at him.

'Sorry Jack.'

William flew through the kitchen into the backyard. Snatching up the hose pipe, he aimed the running water at the coals. Steam and ashes flared up. Next he dashed for the wheelbarrow, leaned it against the boiler and stretched

101

for the safety valve. Jourbor appeared out of the long grass. He beamed a beatific smile as he carried a log of wood. This was a special log that would burn beautifully. Jourbor had hoarded it for just such an occasion, the birth of a river god's child.

He advanced with head down. What a roaring fire he'd build! Suddenly, he saw William on the wheelbarrow. Jourbor dropped the log took a dive at William's legs and pulled him off as the steam escaped from the valve.

William kicked out. 'Let go, you monkey, you want to blow up the bloody house.'

The two men grappled and went down grunting and cursing one another. A small cry came from the bedroom. Both men froze. The cry came again. Liam plopped back into the saddle and Jack looked up the stairs. From the open window, the doctor poked his head out.

'It's a girl,' he squeaked in his high-pitched voice, most unseemly behaviour for a doctor.

The two men stood up, eyed each other for a second. William threw his arms around Jourbor and kissed him on the forehead.

'I have a daughter. I have a daughter,' he yelled and dashed into the house down the passage. 'Sorry Jack.'

William fell on his knees at the bedside, gathered his wife in his arms and smothered her with gentle kisses. 'Are you all right, my darling, are you all right?'

She smiled. 'Very tired.'

The doctor held the baby. William stood up and took the baby in his big hands. 'Are you sure it's a girl?'

This was too much for the good doctor.

'I'll send a nurse,' he told William. '. . . and a male orderly,' eyeing the idiot who thought a doctor did not know the difference between male and female.

Doctor Hasling grabbed his bag and scuttled down the stairs to the wall phone in the passage. As he waited for an answer, he glanced into the kitchen. Jack stood on a chair pouring tea from a large teapot into a brown mug – the colour of his mother's hair. Through the kitchen, the doctor

102

caught a glimpse of the boiler. Smoke and steam billowed up as the black person stoked his fire.

The doctor studied the miniature watercolour on the wall before giving his instructions. Replacing the receiver, he hurried down the passage to the front door. A racket similar to a jackal's howl came from the dining-room. The thin boy cycled around and around the table yelling.

Dr Bert Hasling ran out of the house and climbed into his car. Only then did he become aware of the pony on his side of the hedge. It was kicking up its heels in the bed of dahlias, revelling in its freedom. The doctor squealed. 'There is something about this country, even the bloody horses are demented. Rona Bentwood should have warned me.'

Meanwhile Jack had entered the bedroom. He placed the tea on the bedside table and gave Our Haggerty to his mother.

'For Emma,' he said and smiled down at his little sister.

William came in carrying a painting of the jacaranda tree. Outlined under the tree were two figures. One sitting, the other, seemingly pregnant, stood with an offering in her hand.

Chapter 11

David Bentwood quietly folded the newspaper. Since Hattie's wedding, his dark hair and thick, short beard had become speckled with strands of grey. His bushy eyebrows lifted a fraction as he stared at his feet. What was his wife Rona up to? Her schemes, which usually involved the community, often led to disaster. David heaved his bulk from the chair and pattered to the front door.

At the bottom of the garden the sprinkler snapped a jet of water at irregular intervals. Flowers, shrubs and trees wilted as if asleep in a warm siesta. In the distance, the sounds of the city floated through the afternoon heat.

David stepped into the house and heard a muffled voice coming from the bedroom. He tiptoed to the door and eavesdropped on the one-sided conversation.

'Be a dear,' Rona enunciated her words distinctly. David sucked in his lips. Rona's 'be a dear' prefixed a directive that one dare not refuse. Imagined or not, one felt beholden to Rona.

'. . . Yes, I know that you are busy, but be a dear,' she repeated, 'do have the party at your house. Imagine what your friends will say. How considerate you are. Remember the favour we did for you.'

The monologue continued after a brief pause. David nodded his head, confirming his theory: I told you so. I wonder who the victim will be.

'Of course I'll help,' Rona's voice rose as if affronted. 'I'll invite the women from the bridge club to give a hand. Joan

105

Bekker is a member and she owes me a favour. I will tell her to prepare the main course. Last month I arranged for Doris to care for Joan's children.'

David shook his head. Doris, Joan, Agnes, all these names meant nothing to him. He continued to listen, pressing his head harder against the door.

'Agnes will do the flowers. I'm sure to find someone to provide the desserts. Preparing the snacks won't be too difficult for you, will they? What's that, my dear?'

The eyebrows managed another fraction of an inch. David cocked his ear.

'When . . . what day? Next Friday week, at six-thirty. His Excellency is free that evening . . .'

'Yes dear. I did say the ambassador. Remember to refer to him as HE. That address will be quite in order at social functions and among friends. I have a wonderful surprise for you. Guess who accepted the invitation. Hattie Auston-Jones. I phoned her on the off chance and she said they would love to come. Little Emma is old enough to be left with a babysitter. She said it's time they were more sociable. Now isn't that good news? How privileged you are to have the Auston-Jones accept your invitation. I'll send you a list of other guests.'

David gave the door a gentle push and peeped in. His wife sat at the dressing-table, twisting the telephone cord around her fingers.

'There is no need to thank me, dear. You'll do me a favour one day. Bye.'

David shut the door, tiptoed back to his chair. He was just in time to open the paper before Rona, with her 'no-nonsense' stride came out. She gave a light sniff and tweaked at the hem of her cardigan. This was a ritual that she played out while organising her thoughts. Smoothing her skirt over her buttocks, Rona sat opposite David.

'Dear Betsy Montecland invited us to a cocktail party. It will be held on Friday, a week from today,' Rona said.

David lowered the paper and with a pretence of indifference, inquired, 'Who's the party for?'

106

'For Marion Russell. Although she's been here for quite a while you haven't met her. I'm related to her through my brother's wife's family.'

He decided against questioning for details about the relationship and replied, 'How kind to have . . .'

'They say that her husband threw her out,' Rona interrupted. 'Mind you it is only a rumour, and you know I detest scandal. I must get to the truth.' Rona's cheeks flushed at the injustice of rumours.

'You are a pillar of strength to the community,' said David twitching his paper as if to make his point. 'We certainly need someone like yourself to crush unfounded slander.' He settled his eyebrows back into a natural position.

'I'm a little concerned about her. Marion is an ambitious woman. She'll stop at nothing to get her own way. Maybe if she married again, she'd settle down. Though I must say, she is a very clever young woman. She understands and appreciates art. Her art gallery on Main Street is delightful.'

'I've seen the gallery. The shop next door sells a variety of goods and imported foods.'

'Yes that's the one. I thought Dr Hasling might like to meet Marion. I think they are related, very distant cousins. My brother-in-law's third sister . . .'

David interrupted, his voice overflowing with sweetness: 'You're such a clever matchmaker.'

'I do like to help friends and relations. You remember Hattie Auston-Jones lived with us before she married William.'

'Yes dear, I remember. It was good of you to have her.'

'I enjoy doing little favours for our friends.' Favours and relations were Rona's collectibles. At least the hobby cost David nothing and they kept him amused. David leaned forward and patted her freckled hand.

'You are sincere, and that is important.'

Twilight is momentary in the tropics. When the cloud ceiling hangs low, the darkness is absolute. Night predators awake, preen themselves and slink from their dens. Cacophonies of mysterious rhythms begin. In the cities, street lamps bathe the boulevards in a yellow glow. A nightjar, at home in the city, swoops through the air to find a meal, its eyes are black as the night. The cruel beak stretches wide to snatch flying insects that are drawn against their will to dance in the saffron light.

The traffic slowed to a trickle as the commercial clatter ebbed. A slam of a car door or a click of an iron gate echoed down the street and children called to each other.

The headlights swept over a building.

'Isn't that where Marion Russell lives?' David Bentwood asked Rona as they drove to the party.

'Yes,' replied Rona. 'Her apartment is on the ground floor.'

David slowed. 'Shall we give her a ride to the party?'

'No. We must hurry, as Betsy will need my help.'

Ominous figures darted down the avenues and boulevards. Hungry and angry people loitered in dark corners, waiting for the unwary.

David and Rona arrived at the party as friends and relations of the host drove up. Acquaintances received their invitation because of their wealth or their status in the community.

'There's that rough diamond drinking in the corner,' whispered a guest. 'Toss, er, what's-his-name.'

'My dear, with his wealth, we pardon his vulgarity,' someone replied.

Invitations were sent to one or two educated Africans. They added a little colour to the party. The hostess was honoured if the upper crust of the society, mostly descendants of the pioneers, accepted an invitation.

Charlie Montecland stood at the door welcoming his guests. 'Splendid, come in,' he greeted Dr Hasling, William and Hattie.

Dr Hasling remembered William grappling in the dust with Jourbor at the time of Emma's birth. Often he wanted to ask William if the settlers usually thrash their servants when their wives were in labour.

The party began and the babble of voices increased, until

108

the front door opened. All conversation stopped as Marion Russell made her entrance. Her timing was superb. On the threshold she hesitated for a moment, enough time to hear an intake of breath, a whisper, an envious sigh. She held still, poised with dignity. Her backless dress hinting at the inviting curves of her breasts and hips, reached just below the knees. Narrow sandals accentuated her long legs sheathed in fine silk. From under carefully shaped eyebrows Marion's green eyes surveyed the room. She stood erect, vibrant and satisfied, then continued down into the sunken lounge.

Charlie Montecland bounced among the guests as fast as etiquette allowed. He wanted to tuck Marion's hand under his arm and parade around the room. Unfortunately for him, Rona Bentwood got to the door first.

She touched cheeks with Marion and said, 'My dear, how nice to see you.'

'Daaarling,' answered Marion in return.

Rona gushed on. 'My dear, you must meet the doctor. Now where is he ... never mind, later. Come, I'll introduce you to William Auston-Jones. He owns the big house, the white one with columns. His grandfather was in diamonds.'

The older woman held Marion's hand as they squeezed through the guests.

'Excuse us, excuse us.' Rona ploughed a path through the crowd.

They avoided hands clutching drinks. They squeezed past guests without touching bodies or tipping waiters' trays. Inconsequential chatter rose and fell.

'Wonderful weather,' bellowed a guest.

'... Rains soon.' A squeak came from his elbow. 'The farmers need rain for the tobacco crops.'

'My dear, my new cookboy, he's marvellous.' Mrs Betsy Montecland's smile stretched over her protruding teeth.

Marion pulled Rona's hand as they made their way to the open patio doors. 'Who is that handsome man standing by the window?'

Rona glanced to the left. 'Isaac M'kama. Come on.'

'My God! He is magnificent!' Marion murmured. 'Truly

109

he looks like the lion of Africa standing there against the night sky.'

Overhead lightning zigzagged through the gathering storm clouds. In the garden the hedges and shrubs leaned like ghostly shapes.

Two men stood by the patio door, their heads bent in earnest talk. The taller man faced the assembled guests. He looked up for a moment and exclaimed:

'Oh bugger it, William! Here comes Rona Bentwood barging along like a tug out of water. Christ, Betsy Montecland is following her. She looks like a bloody ostrich with teeth. Look at her head bobbing. I'm out.'

'Bloody hell, Toss. Don't leave me with them,' William laughed and snatched at his companion's arm but he was too late. Toss slipped through the patio door.

Rona Bentwood halted at William's side.

'Oh William my dear, do meet Marion Russell. William's an artist; I'm sure you will have much in common.' She patted his sleeve. 'Marion has opened her own art gallery.'

'It's the boutique next to that cute little shop, you know on High Street.' Betsy Montecland chipped in. 'The manager imports such delightful items. I've seen you in there, William. Buying "smalls" for your wife, you naughty man.'

Rona ignored the interruption. 'We'll leave you two together. Oh, there is your wife.' The group glanced in Hattie's direction.

Hattie, her features partly obscured by her brown hair, was speaking to an acquaintance. '. . . That's correct,' she was saying, '. . . branch off at The Junction. I lived near there as a child. My brother Seth farms there now. The silly goof,' a dimpled smile quickly came and went, 'prospects for gold in his spare time.'

While Hattie spoke, Marion quickly summed up William's status. A wealthy man who wears evening dress with casual elegance, she thought. Probably bored with his mousey wife standing across the room. I wonder . . .

'Charmed, I'm sure.' William interrupted Marion's

110

thoughts as he acknowledged the introduction with a slight bow. 'Those who like me call me William, would you?'

William had found his model.

'Like you – or call you William?' smiled the beautiful Marion. She winked shyly and her thigh muscles contracted suggestively.

William grinned and opened his hand, gesturing a question. 'Both, I wish. Do you have plenty of art supplies? I never have enough.'

'I'm sure I have all your needs.'

'I'm sure you have . . .'

David Bentwood appeared as if from nowhere.

'My dear fellow,' he haw-hawed, and took William's arm. 'Come with me young fellow, I've a bone to pick with you. Haven't seen you and your good lady for years.' He pulled William into the centre of the room.

'Shit,' Marion swore quietly, 'bloody pompous ass.'

'Eat! Madam?' A tray of wilting snacks appeared under her nose. The waiter in squeaky white uniform offered his wares with an insinuating grin. Marion shook her head.

'Madam?' he persisted with a false smile. She waved him away. Several male guests came up to talk with her. She laughed with them, lowered her eyelashes, stirred a thigh and watched them squirm. Charlie Montecland wished his wife could do that – flutter her eyelids and wiggle her fanny.

Rona Bentwood approached Marion and said, 'There is something I must tell you.'

'Some other time. I must speak with my hosts before I leave. Early start tomorrow.' Marion slipped away.

The waiter mingled among the guests then walked over and offered his tray to his half-brother, Isaac. Without greeting his relation, Isaac filled his mouth with snacks and sipped his whisky. 'Is that Marion Russell who was talking to William Auston-Jones?'

'Yes, probably after his money. Her business is failing. My friend who works for her told me,' answered the waiter.

'Is that so?' said Isaac. He glanced around the room making mental notes of the guests.

111

Isaac's eye caught Hattie's diamond clasp – it was the most beautiful jewel he had ever seen. Isaac became oblivious to all as he remembered his boyhood. He recalled the raindrop, it was so round and so clear on the wild marigold. He saw shafts of the sun's rays dancing on the river. He recalled a sparkling world, a land glittering like a jewel in morning dew. A land of jewels that he longed to own.

'Are you having fun, Isaac?' Betsy Montecland sneaked up behind him.

As Isaac was so suddenly brought back to reality, he started. Perspiration was running down his temple. Quickly, he wiped his face with a white handkerchief and focused his eyes on the woman beside him. A swift thought slipped through his mind: why would a man want to fuck a dame with big teeth?

He bowed respectfully and answered. 'A delightful party, thank you, madam.' Again he glanced quickly at the diamond brooch and the person who wore it with such grace.

'How are your children?' Betsy patronised him.

'All eighteen children are very well. Thank you for asking.'

Taken aback as she was, Betsy soldiered on. 'Have you tried one of these?' She held a soggy portion of bread in her bony fingers. 'Do try it.'

'No thank you, I don't eat little black seeds.'

'Oh, my goodness,' giggled Betsy, 'don't be so silly. They're not seeds! It's caviar, a white man's delicacy. When you're civilised Isaac, you'll enjoy them.' She giggled again.

Ignorant bitch, Isaac thought. His brown eyes hardened with hatred. 'I'm sure I will. Now if you will excuse me, I must get home to my four wives. I must bed them all tonight.' He banged his glass on a passing tray.

'Oh,' blushed Betsy taken back. 'I . . . I . . . Are all your wives keeping well?'

'Witless hag,' Isaac answered, and turning his back on her, he walked away.

As Isaac left the party the insult rang through his mind. 'When he became civilised . . .' He wanted revenge. Stalking

112

through the patio door, he crossed the lawn and pushed through the hedge.

Thunder rumbled and big drops of rain hit the ground. In the driveway he saw Marion start her car and pull out. He remembered his mother saying, 'Keep Marion Russell in mind.'

Isaac followed Marion from a safe distance until she entered her driveway. He slowed to a stop, and watched her enter the house. After waiting a few moments, he climbed out of the car. In spite of his bulk, Isaac moved with the grace and stealth of the big cats. He stepped on to the porch and pushed the door. It swung open.

Dumb woman leaving her door unlocked, Isaac thought. I hope she'll be the answer to my problem.

Marion stood in front of a wall mirror. Her hair, released from confinement hung to her waist. She was searching for signs of wrinkles between her brows when Isaac's image appeared over her shoulder. She smiled then faced him. His eyes mirrored no emotion from the depth of their deep sockets as he held out his arms.

When Isaac returned to his own house, the dull day had dawned.

Chapter 12

Unlocking the gallery door with the rusted key was another irritating problem that plagued Marion Russell. The extreme heat, unpaid bills and her employee's demands taxed her patience and her strength. Isaac's late-night visits left her feeling uneasy, as if their sexual relationship was contrived. He continually urged her to meet William. Marion regretted ever encouraging Rona Bentwood's weekly visit to the gallery. Her admiration for Dr Hasling sickened and annoyed Marion.

'He's so conscientious,' Rona gushed, 'and dedicated to his research in tropical diseases. What a wonderful husband he will be.' Receiving no comment, Rona continued with her idle chatter. Marion abhorred gossip and prattle which she thought stuck like grime. Filth leads to squalor and deprivation. She had lived in poverty throughout her childhood and now, as an adult, she vowed never to exist under those circumstances again.

If only all her misgivings could be unlocked like a door, thought Marion, jiggling the key again when William pulled up at the kerb and climbed from the car.

'Here, allow me to help you.'

Taking the key from her, he forced the lock and the door clicked open.

'Thanks. You've rescued me.'

William followed her into the gallery and stopped by a painting.

'Gabriel, who would that be? I didn't know there was an artistic archangel around here.'

'A youth delivered the work yesterday. Said his father would come by later.'

'Gabriel. Gabriel, I thought I knew all the local painters.'

'When I meet the mysterious artist, I'll let you know. What are you doing here in the heat of the day?'

'My wife threw me out, said I was interfering with the children. She told me to find my own toys, or the model I am always going on about. She and the children live in a world of their own making. I lost at dominoes last night.'

'You lost at a childish game! That's not a tragedy.'

'Of course not but Hattie assumes . . .' His explanations dwindled off as he contemplated the other works of art.

Eventually, he sauntered over to the glass counter. 'So here I am looking for a model. Will you sit for me?'

After a moment, he ran his fingers over her cheek and under the collar of her silk blouse.

'I like to get to know my subjects. Feel the formation of muscles and bone,' he said. 'Your bone structure is perfect and the texture of your flesh is flawless. I . . .'

'You . . . hoo,' interrupted a voice from the doorway.

William still leaning across the counter twisted around and exclaimed. 'Oh Christ! Betsy Montecland the bloody town crier and busybody to boot.' Bending further over the counter, he declared in a loud voice. 'That's the size of the canvas I need.'

Marion stepped aside and looked over his shoulder.

'That's quick thinking. You may have fooled her,' she whispered to him.

'You . . . hoo Betsy.' Marion returned the wave.

'Buying paints, are you?' Betsy Montecland's voice entered the gallery. 'Buying more paints. My, William, you do paint too much and your pictures are so pretty. All those darling little animals frolicking about and butterflies resting on the flowers. Hattie showed me a painting the other day. I came collecting for the little black children's Christmas treat. This

116

coming Christmas we'll give them golliwogs. They'll love that. Yes Hattie showed me your pretty picture.'

'I'll murder Hatts if she does that again,' William whispered through clenched teeth.

'You have bought more "smalls" for your wifey from the cute little shop next door.' Betsy pointed to a slim package in William's pocket with an arthritic finger. 'I must fly. No time to chat. I've work to do, not like the idle rich. My friends are coming in for coffee. Wednesday is my "At Home" afternoon. I shall tell them I saw you two together. Tomorrow is my bridge morning.' She toddled on her high heels out the door, the two feathers in her hat bobbed.

'Buying from that cute little shop, silly old bat,' mimicked William as he drew a sheet of notepaper from his back pocket. His shirt sleeves rolled up to the elbows exposed the fine golden hairs curling on his forearms.

'Here is a list of paints, if you have them let me know and I'll collect them later,' he said flicking the paper between two long fingers.

Marion took the list from him. 'Sure, and I will find out who "Gabriel" is.'

'I see you're exhibiting Africans' arts and crafts.'

'Yes. They've a unique talent, so refreshing and distinctive. I'm hoping to start a lucrative market for their work. The work I shipped overseas has received encouraging results.'

'It's time someone recognised their talents, instead of imposing our traditions on them. Collecting for the little black childrens' Christmas party. What do they know or care about golliwogs. Their bellies are empty most of the year. Betsy Montecland, the silly bitch, would do better if she left them alone.'

Marion touched his arm. 'What are you working on now?'

'I've just completed a study. Now I'm experimenting with a different technique. I need advice and someone to discuss it with.'

'Bring your canvas into the gallery, I'd love to see it.'

'You'll have to come to the house. Hatts won't let any of my paintings leave the house.'

117

'Why?'

'She says the right time is not yet; we must wait until I'm completely satisfied with my work. Besides, she tells me that they're too personal and refers to them as "love letters". Who can argue with that?' William explained throwing up his hands.

'That is touching but I hope to see and market your work.'

'I know what. Come over any day and look at them. Stay for lunch. The place is easy to find, just follow the signs to Pioneer Hill. Grey stone pillars mark the entrance to the house.'

'Thanks. I'll take up your offer.'

'I must go,' smiled William. 'Hattie will be wondering if I have fallen off the edge of the earth. Yes, I better hurry. I don't trust that slave of hers. Jourbor worships Hattie like a personal goddess. I'm sure he wants to sacrifice her to redeem his lost soul.'

'William, surely you exaggerate.'

'Only a little.'

William gave a small salute and left quickly.

Standing just inside the door Marion watched him go. Traffic noises and native voices swelled and diminished. She deliberated. Strange country of eccentric people, they seem so restless – always on the move. For no apparent reason she remembered Isaac. Why did he want her to meet William? Well, she would not tell him her own reasons. Men like William were easy prey.

Three days later with William's invitation, 'Come to see us any time,' echoing in her thoughts, Marion started on a path to fulfil her selfish desires. She dressed with care, smart yet casual. The costume she chose hinted of a country style, casual slacks, silk blouse and lightweight jacket. A chiffon scarf held her dark hair and stressed the plane of her cheekbones and forehead. A touch of rouge skilfully applied drew the eyes from the narrow bridged nose. Ever fashion conscious, she achieved a cool and sophisticated appearance.

She scolded herself as she drove her blue sedan. Don't be

condescending or patronising to Hattie, the plain little mother hen. Probably she lives in a world of fantasy and she considers herself some sort of goddess worshipped by her servant Jourbor. Poor William, sympathised Marion, living with a person with little or no intellect.

'I shall be careful not to cause any jealousy,' Marion told herself. Confrontation with Hattie could come later when her emotions would be of little consequence.

Marion appraised art with sincerity and integrity. Her reputation as an art dealer depended on her honesty. She decided to critique William's work candidly but also be supportive and encouraging.

Following the clearly marked signs to Pioneer Hill she came to the stone pillars with a discreet copper plaque. Marion turned into the tree-lined drive that led to the house.

Without warning a horse and rider appeared from nowhere. Marion panicked, yanking the steering wheel hard over. She screamed as the car hit the tree. The windshield cracked into thousands of splinters. Abruptly the rider, the horse and swaying branches melted into a distorted mass of swirling colours before her eyes. Marion fell unconscious over the steering wheel.

The throbbing ache that brought her back to reality felt as if a blacksmith was shoeing an elephant. Bright colours spiralled to a diminishing point at the back of her eyes. Her mouth felt dry as an emery board. Gradually the turmoil of colour dissolved into a neutral mist. Footsteps like the sound of sneakers came from somewhere on her left. Marion groaned and lifted her head. The footsteps ceased immediately and a voice spoke from a distance.

'Thank God you're okay.'

Marion tried to answer but the pain increased and the mist behind her eyes thickened. Again the voice called, this time more urgently.

'Marion, Marion.'

A warm and comforting hand on her shoulder persuaded her to open her eyes. William leaned over her, his expression full of concern.

119

'Where am I? What happened?' she asked in a dry voice. 'I remember a swaying branch and a galloping horse.'

'You're in the hospital; you sideswiped a tree and hit your head on the dash.' William spoke softly, as if he knew how her head hurt. 'Your car's in the repair shop, the damage is slight, and I'll meet the expenses. Rest now. Sister Purdy will be with you in a moment.'

Marion closed her eyes, grateful to sink into oblivion. By the following morning her recovery was almost complete. Although pale, she lay back in bed looking most attractive. Her dark hair contrasted with the white pillows and the flowers at her bedside. Through the curtained window she saw the extensive hospital grounds. Tropical shrubs, bougainvillaea, hibiscus and syringa in full bloom edged the velvet green lawns.

William entered, carrying another bouquet and several magazines.

'Hello there, feeling better? Hattie sent these. She hopes they are to your liking. If there is anything you want, let us know.'

'I've all I need, besides I'll be going home tomorrow. Thank Hattie for me,' Marion managed a small smile. 'Tell me what happened yesterday. I can't remember.'

'My son Liam, the thoughtless knave, he caused your accident. He mistook your car for his uncle's. Both the cars are dark blue. When Seth, his uncle, comes for a visit, they race each other along the drive. It's a game of theirs. They'll never play it again, Hattie will make sure of that.'

William leaned against the window frame. His tanned body contrasted with his immaculate white drills and open-necked shirt. One day soon, Marion envisaged, as she watched him recalling the previous day's events, she would know the strength of his arms about her.

'What did Hattie say?' Marion asked.

'She was infuriated.' William grinned at the recollection. 'She cornered me and Liam in the dining-room this morning.'

120

After breakfast Hattie ordered Liam and William to remain in the room.

She began her tirade with Liam. 'You should use the sense you were born with.' Liam hung his head and scuffed his runners.

'God's strewth. Hattie is furious,' William muttered under his breath. Anger had brought up the colour in her cheeks and eyes. Laboured breathing raised and lowered her breast. He saw the outline of firm nipples under the fabric of her blouse. Remembering the taste of them, he wetted his lips. How provocative and desirable she was. After twelve years of marriage and intimacy, she still excited him.

Hattie started on her husband. 'Wipe that silly grin off your face, this is not a laughing matter, William. You assured me Liam could control that pony.'

William squirmed and tried to conceal his desire. 'He can . . .'

'. . . But I didn't disobey Dad,' interrupted Liam. 'I'm allowed to gallop my pony, Frith, Dad said so. I never went off the estate.'

'Liam, I want no excuses – tie your laces,' Hattie ordered.

The boy lifted his foot and hopped about and managed half a pretzel knot – it became undone before his foot hit the floor. No one noticed.

'I thought it was Uncle Seth; his car is also blue,' Liam wailed. 'We always race up the drive.'

'Your Uncle Seth has no more sense than your father. He'll get it from me when I see him again. As soon as Mrs Russell comes out of the hospital you will go and apologise.'

While Hattie gave her instructions, William edged Liam out the door.

'Get out,' he whispered through a clenched mouth. 'I'll try to calm your mother.'

Liam, partially protected by his father, reached the door then scuttled away down the passage, slamming the screen door behind him.

William shuddered. 'I must do something about that door,'

121

he promised, then added. 'Don't you think you're being too severe?'

Hattie charged him again. 'Don't sympathise with Liam. The horse might have reared and Liam been thrown under the wheels of the car. What then! He must learn not to be so foolish. You can take him to apologise.'

'Very well, I will take him. It's a shame, to punish him like that.'

'His punishment will absolve his guilt. I don't want Liam living with remorse. Seth never forgave himself for his childhood mistakes.'

Moving closer to Marion's bed, William said. 'Hattie has inflicted dreadful punishment on the boy. I feel a mite sorry for the lad.'

'Oh William! The poor boy, please tell Hattie to forgive him. I already have,' Marion pleaded prettily.

William snorted. 'Don't worry, our ideas of punishment are very different from his.'

'What will happen to him?'

'When you are back at the gallery, he will come to apologise.'

Marion raised her neatly arched eyebrows. 'Is that a fitting punishment?'

'Not in itself. The worst punishment that can befall young Liam is to make him bathe in the middle of the day. When he comes to apologise, he must dress in his best suit. He will wear his Sunday suit actually.'

'That's his punishment, to be clean and neatly dressed?'

'Yes, all spruced up,' repeated William. 'That will be agony for him, he'll feel a right Charlie.'

A whipping would be more appropriate. These wealthy people are indulgent, can't they discipline their children, thought Marion, if ever I have control over him it'll be a different story.

'I'm in trouble as well,' William tried to look contrite. 'I have to bring him with the other two, Jack and Emma.

Grubby little devils, they are. I never know what mischief they'll get up to.'

Marion smiled wanly. 'Well at least I'll meet your children. I am looking forward to the pleasure.'

'Yes, it'll be mine as well.' He winked at her. 'See you later.'

Chapter 13

An elderly nurse waddled into the ward. Her starched uniform crackled as she puffed the pillows and smoothed the sheets with deft hands.

'There you are, that's more comfortable,' said Sister Purdy. 'My, the flowers are beautiful. Did Hattie send them, she's so kind and thoughtful. William insisted we nurse you with extra loving care.'

Marion smiled her thanks. Her scheme was falling in place quicker than she expected. William's actions and thoughtfulness showed promise of an intimate relationship.

'He rode with you in the ambulance. What a tizz he was in. The hospital staff is familiar with William's hysteria. He is so protective and anxious with his loved ones.'

The sister placed her hand on her ample hip and pressed her thighs against the bed and continued talking.

'I remember about a year ago. He came dashing through the swing doors carrying his son Jack in his arms. What a rumpus he caused by shouting orders at the staff on the ward. Mind you, the boy's wound looked life-threatening. Cuts on the chin do bleed badly. William had the nurses in an uproar by demanding the attention of the chief surgeon. No one else, William made it clear, qualified for his son's needs. Poor Dr Hasling coming through the door took one look and yelled, "Crazy man, he is bloody crazy." He scuttled down the corridor which is so unlike the staid doctor.'

'What happened then?'

'Jack eventually calmed his father down. Now what did

125

the boy say? Oh yes, I remember, "Stop flapping, Dad." We all laughed and Hattie managed to coax her husband out of the surgery.'

The sister tucked a strand of grey hair under her starched linen cap.

'Surely the child was in agony?' said Marion.

'Well yes. Having stitches is painful.'

'Poor little mite,' Marion commiserated sweetly. 'Are you friends of the Auston-Jones?'

'I have known them for years. Charming people, they are. My husband's parents and William's were early settlers. They all suffered so much tragedy during the early years. William's family more than most.' Sister Purdy became serious for a moment. 'You know, we can't decide if the country makes the nation or the nation is the country. Both are young, inexperienced and uncertain of the path to take.' Giving the bedcover a final pat, she added with a laugh, 'Unyielding they are, but oh my, so virile.'

A shadow darkened the doorway. Sister Purdy at the bedside whipped around and glared at the smartly dressed African standing there holding a pathetic bunch of wilted snapdragons. A piece of crumpled foil protected the stems.

'What are you doing here?' the sister curtly addressed the man. 'This is the European hospital. The African wards are around the other side of the building.'

'Please Sister,' said Isaac submissively, 'I have brought these flowers for Madam. Her workers, the ones who carve her statues, sent them. Thank you, Sister.' Raising his straw hat, he bowed slightly.

'Isaac, do come in,' exclaimed Marion. 'How kind of you to visit me.' Without bothering to cover her naked shoulders Marion sat up and held out her hand.

The nurse looked disgustedly at Marion's lack of propriety and intimate manner with Isaac. 'The bell is above the bed. Ring if you need anything,' she said harshly.

Sister Purdy's intolerance and racial attitude filled Isaac with hatred; one day he'd retaliate. She ignored his satirical bow and mocking grin as she brushed past him. He watched

126

her disappear into the next ward before approaching Marion's bedside.

'Isaac, I'm ashamed of the sister's rude manners. I expected more racial tolerance from her,' Marion said.

Isaac threw the flowers onto a chair and perched one buttock on the bed. He inspected his palms and then maliciously he wiped them on the bedcover.

'Your assistant at your gallery told me about your mishap.' He spoke in disjointed phrases. 'Next time I'll stay the night; you'll want me to. That'll cause a scandal.'

'I don't want any talk or gossip. I can't afford to lose any more customers.'

'Sure I know, but I want something from you.'

'Anything within reason.' Marion gave a coy smile and immediately felt ridiculous as he pulled down his mouth at her reply.

'The three exhibits on display in the gallery. I told your assistant to keep them aside for me.' Isaac glanced around the room. He appreciated the tranquillity and order in the ward.

'You must pay the artists, it's their livelihood.'

Isaac flicked his wrist, dismissing her concern. 'Don't worry about them, they produce that stuff by the ton. That's all they do and it's a tedious job for them. When we have our independence they won't need to work so hard. Besides, right now my needs are more important. I heard you had this accident on Auston-Jones's property. What were you doing there?'

'He invited me to see his work.'

'Good. You're getting on familiar terms with William.' Isaac nodded his head with satisfaction and repeated. 'That's good.'

'Why are you insisting that I get to know him?'

'I've my reasons and my plans.'

'What are your reasons? If I'm involved I'd like to know.'

'Later, some other time I'll tell you.'

'Have you seen his paintings?'

'My sister, Gladys has. She said the animals in the pictures

127

look alive and at any moment will spring from the wall. The flowers and trees grow each day. Remember though, Gladys is a simple girl.'

'Have you any idea why Hattie keeps them from the public?'

'I don't know. That family keep their secrets and business to themselves. I must go now, we'll get together soon and talk about our schemes.' He left the ward moving across the floor on light steps.

Marion reached over to gather the wilted flowers and pushed them into a vase close by. Isaac's visit frightened her. What was his purpose, blackmail? No, she laughed at her fears, why would he blackmail her. After all, racial barriers worked both ways. Isaac was different from other men. Probably, he had nothing as a child and knows no better. She and Isaac were alike, both ambitious and smart enough to achieve their goals. What a striking pair they would make as leaders of a newly independent country. Together with their drive and intelligence they would build a nation in peace and harmony. First she must be solvent and her business thriving.

Marion lay back thinking of her next move. William, he was the answer. Somehow she'll ensnare him and get her hands on his wealth. She'd use any means to achieve her aims; manipulate his children, his wife or his emotions. And it might be enjoyable sleeping with him.

Chapter 14

With his hands pressed on the handbasin William raised his head and saw Hattie's reflection in the mirror. Her image revealed the melancholy in her face. She listlessly stroked the door frame.

'Liam must apologise to Mrs Russell,' she said. 'I hurt to see my son so unhappy but I must not relent now.'

Hattie sighed and came into the bathroom. 'He's bathed and dressed and is waiting. Jack and Emma are going with you. They wouldn't miss this drama for the world.'

'Why must I take the other two?' William asked woefully. He turned on the taps, bent over and splashed water over his face.

Hattie stepped up behind him and locked her hands around his waist. For a moment or two, with her cheek pressed against his shoulder blades, she listened to his heart beat.

'I love you dearly,' she said.

'I don't believe you. How can you possibly love me when you insist I take those leprechauns in the Jag?' William reached for a hand towel and dried his face and hands. Tossing the towel into the handbasin, he twisted around.

'Hm, tell me that,' he said and held her by the shoulders. 'You want to be rid of us. No doubt you and your self-appointed slave are going to make that dreadful gooseberry jam.'

Hattie's eyes twinkled. 'You'll have something more exciting than jam when you come home.' She rose on tiptoes and kissed him. 'I love you,' she said again.

William chuckled. 'You're a hot . . .'

'Yes, I know. The children are in the Jag. You must hurry as Emma will get into mischief.'

'Emma in the Jag! Dear God no.' He dashed from the bathroom.

'Jack's with her,' shouted Hattie when she managed to control her laughter.

The two children, with faces freshly washed and hair combed, sat in the back. Jack wore his Sunday suit and favourite tie. He felt he must support his brother. William glanced at their innocent faces and then he surveyed the seats for signs of small grubby handprints. There were none, so he climbed into the car and looked across at Liam.

The window framed the boy's head and slender physique. In his hands, strong enough to control a galloping pony, he gently held a nosegay of violets. Dark green leaves that formed a border around the posy, contrasting with the deep purple flowers.

Liam sat very still. His appearance had altered during the past three years. His features were in perfect proportion with the shape of the face. Flowers and childhood fade, reflected William. The essence of childhood was as fleeting as the fragrance of violets.

Hattie's guess was wrong. The boy was not half of William. He was all of his mother. From her, he inherited two characteristics, integrity and loyalty. Like her, he was free spirited, born to ride on the wind or to skip through the clouds. William remembered Hattie dancing with his arms about her waist. Twelve years ago they had cavorted around the garden. Her hair swirling freely, her step unfettered and her spirits soaring in the warm evening air.

Emma's whispering, 'Have you got the candy, Jack?' shattered William's memory.

'Oh no you don't, my young lady,' William stretched his arm over the back seat. 'No candy in my Jag. Give it to me, Jack, you may have it when we get there.'

130

Liam gave a little smile. William saw it and his soul filled with pride. This is *my* son. He tenderly pressed the boy's shoulder then started the car.

William carried Emma and held Jack's hand as they crossed the street. At the door of the gallery he put her down and threatened her and Jack with grisly punishment if they dared move from that spot.

'Move just one inch, I'll paint every part of your body, young Jack, with thick black greasy paint. Then I'll snip off every hair on your head with the hedge clippers.'

Although he looked menacing, he did not deceive the children. His threats were more amusing than frightening.

'And you, Miss,' he looked down at a little red pouting lips and two brown eyes widening with expectation. Fair curls framed Emma's face. Her bonnet hung at the back of her head.

'What are you going to do to me, Daddy?' she asked hopping from one foot to the other.

'Parcel you up and send you to the pixies.' He tickled her tummy.

'By bus. Like Mummy sends parcels to Uncle Seth?'

'Yes by bus. With stamps pinned on you. Big red stamps made from gold. Now both stay here. Eat your candy.'

The children giggled at their father's threats and happily waited, with their heads poking around the door.

Inside the gallery, Liam scuffed his shoes and handed the nosegay to Marion. She lowered her long eyelashes seductively at William as Liam mumbled his apology.

'He looks silly standing there,' whispered Jack.

'She is holding his hand! Where's she taking him?' asked Emma. Both children leaned further into the gallery. They could see and hear Marion talking to Liam in a corner.

'Let's play a trick on your father,' she said. 'I want you to hide a tube of purple paint. I'll put it in the packet. We'll send him on a treasure hunt.'

Liam had enough of games and thought this a rather silly idea. Yet he must obey her. He didn't want to wear this suit for the rest of his life. She noticed his hesitation.

131

'Here,' she held out a pound note. Liam inherited his good luck from his grandfather. Fortunes came looking for them.

'Okay,' he said nonchalantly and pocketed the money.

'That's a good boy. Go back to your father.'

Marion reached out her hand to ruffle his hair but Liam dodged the long manicured nails. Elegantly, she walked back to the counter, and placed several tubes of paints in a packet and handed it to William.

'These complete your order,' she said.

'Thanks. Hold this Liam, while I fix this account,' said William and dipped his hand into his pocket.

Liam took the packet, opened it and withdrew a tube. He looked about for a moment then dropped it under the counter then squashed the tube with his foot. The cap popped off and paint streaked out in a perfect curve.

Emma squealed with delight. William looked up, but Jack quickly pulled her away from the door and covered her mouth.

'Come Liam, let's hurry. I don't trust those monkeys, they're up to something.'

'Bye Mrs Russell,' called Liam and gave her a charming smile.

Two hours later William phoned. 'Sorry to bother you Marion, but one tube of paint is missing. Have you another?'

'Yes, at home,' she explained, 'could you fetch it sometime?'

'How about tomorrow? I know it's Saturday afternoon but that's about the only time I could make it. Hattie takes the children to the gymkhana.'

'That's fine by me. Come about three.'

Marion mused as she prepared for the Saturday afternoon visit. William was pliable and gullible as a puppet. Pull a string and he jumps, Marion mused. She sprayed the room with air freshener. 'Lilies of the Field' the label read on the canister. The arrangements of imported tulips graced the coffee table. Marion checked the tray of drinks and plate of snacks. The stage was set for his visit. Perfect.

132

An hour went by and William had not yet arrived. Marion became increasingly annoyed as she paced the floor. Men didn't normally keep her waiting. She was about to throw out the snacks when the doorbell rang. Unhurriedly, she replaced the plate on the tray, checked her makeup in the wall mirror, then went to the door.

'Sorry I'm late but Miss Poppet caused my delay,' William said when Marion opened the door. 'I had to bring her. She wanted to crawl under the horses.'

Marion looked down at the mischievous toddler. Oh God! Marion panicked. The tulips on the table, they cost a fortune. With an effort she controlled her disappointment.

'Well you're here now, come in.'

'I think not. Look at her,' he answered, 'sucking on that barley sugar. The room will be a sticky mess in no time. She is such a grubby little miss. The next time she rides in the Jag will be on her wedding day.'

Emma removed the candy from her mouth, inspected it and deciding it would last for a long while, put it back into her mouth.

'Well we . . . another time.' William's intonation suggested more than a casual visit.

'Yes, of course, but come in. It will be okay.'

'Only for a moment.'

Emma licked her lips as she looked up at Marion. The woman shuddered and stepped aside.

'I see they stopped building those apartments,' said William glancing through the window. 'There is no incentive to expand with all this political upheaval.'

'Please sit. What can I get you to drink, martini, beer?'

William perched himself on the edge of the armchair and drew his daughter into the circle of his arms. 'Not now thanks, too early.'

'I'll get your paints, won't be a moment.' Marion left the room.

William thanked Marion when she returned with a package. 'I'd better take this child to her Gladys, that's her nanny,

133

for a bath and change of clothing. What do you say?' he asked the child.

'Nanny, barf,' she answered.

'Yes, you need a barf,' he smiled at the child. 'Then we will go back to Mama and your brothers. They'll be missing you.'

He raised his head and said to Marion. 'Hattie and the children are inseparable; at times I feel like an outsider.' William caressed the child and continued. 'Hattie's not feeling too well although she is on medication.'

He lifted Emma off his lap and stood up. Marion handed him the small package.

'How much do I owe you?'

'Don't worry about it now. Pay when you come into the gallery again.'

'Sure. Come Poppet, let's go.' He took the child's hand and went to the door. 'Thanks, see you later.'

The clock chimed five. What a waste of a Saturday afternoon. Marion had expected them to make their way to her bed, if not at least have had a stimulating conversation. Bloody tulips, he didn't even notice them. Yet she learned something positive. He's lonely in his own home. He needs a friend with the same standard of intellect.

A week went by before William found himself at the country hotel. Although the establishment had become rather seedy over the years, it still held pleasant memories for him. Weeds had replaced the flowering shrubs and displaced bricks, which had formed a serrated edge of the flower-beds, lay in an untidy pile. Strips of faded paint hung from the door.

Two days ago Marion had phoned to tell him she had met the mysterious Gabriel. He wanted to meet a fellow artist.

Marion suggested that maybe the three of them meet late one afternoon.

'Did you mention my name?' William had asked.

'No. I wanted to surprise him. I said you were a stranger in town.'

134

William entered the dining-room and glanced about. A waiter came forward and pointed to a table near the window. Nearby three or four couples sat chatting over their dinner. The waiter held out a menu.

'Not just yet,' William said. 'I'm waiting for another party. Ah, there she is. Bring me a bottle of wine.'

Diners turned their heads to watch Marion glide past. At the table William seated her and then sat opposite with his back to the centre of the room.

'I'm still in a flurry, I can't wait to meet your mysterious artist.' William poured her a glass of wine.

'He'll be here soon. By the way I've booked a room. I don't like driving on my own at night.'

'Very sensible of you. Let's eat while we wait.' William suggested.

As Marion studied the menu, she sensed his stare. She glanced up. How wealthy is he, wondered Marion. After tonight I'll know.

'The evening light accents the composition of your throat and shoulders,' William said. 'As an artist I must capture the feel of colour and composition.'

'You will be able to.'

'How?'

'Through your fingers.'

'May I touch your face?'

Marion clinched her teeth. Dear God! Has he no motivation or is he so naïve?

He reached over and smoothed her cheek. His fingers strayed over her throat and across her shoulders. Suddenly, he stopped his exploring and listened.

'Do you hear that?'

'No. What?'

'African drums.'

'No. I hear your heart.'

He ignored her remarks.

'Listen,' he repeated.

The drumming grew louder and was more urgent.

'Jourbor interprets the voice of the drums. He told Hattie

135

the drums send important news.' William got up and went close to the window, listening. Marion pushed back her chair and walked out of the hotel to her car.

'Why can't he make up his mind? It's Hattie, Hattie all the time. He really loves that plain brown hen.'

Slapping her hand on the steering wheel, she vowed, 'One day I'll get him. If he's fooling with me, he'll regret it. I'll make him pay.'

William came out of his reverie and looked around for Marion. At that moment Toss walked in.

'What are you doing here, old man?' he called and joined William at the table.

'I'm not sure. Anyhow have a drink.' William pointed to the waiter. 'Is he one of your sons?'

Toss glanced back at the dark-skinned waiter.

'He could be,' he answered quite composed. 'I can't keep track of all my offspring. My women are always popping them out.'

William shook his head as if despairing for the man.

'Just heard the drums, Toss. Can you understand what they are drumming about?'

'Nothing in particular as far as I can tell. Rabble rousers are supplying the beer. Looking for support for their party. Most of the people have no idea about a democratic vote, why should they? Through the centuries they accepted tribal ruling, no matter who or the colour of their skin. Their system of governing worked for them. Voting means nothing to them. They will vote for anyone who supplies them with free liquor, and so would I.'

Toss frowned and searched the room with his eyes. 'A sexy dame was to meet me here. She said she wanted me to meet a colleague. I wonder where she is?'

William's mouth dropped open as he rose from the table. He pointed to Toss and began to babble.

'You . . .' he choked. 'You . . . are Gabriel, named after an angel! Why didn't you tell me and our pals your proper name when we were at school?'

'What!' yelled Toss, 'Tell a gang of little heathens my real

136

name and be ridiculed ever afterwards. I wasn't that daft. And no, before you ask, I tell you. I don't know why or who named me, Toss.'

Holding his sides and roaring with laughter, William staggered from the room.

'Gabriel McPhearson. Gabriel . . . bloody . . . McPhearson.' He reached the path and put his foot on the statue. The same statue that he once described as a constipated bird or an angel. It had toppled over.

William's mirth continued. 'I must tell Hattie. I must tell Hattie.'

Never again would William laugh so joyfully or with such abandon.

Chapter 15

Who could be hurrying down the street in the stifling heat? A youth, hearing the sharp tattoo of high heels on the concrete glanced over his shoulder. What urgent tidings could the elderly lady carry? He nudged his companions who followed his glance then jeered and laughed.

Everything – the air, the plants and passers-by seemed brittle and lethargic in the blistering heat. Day after day, dark clouds, swollen with moisture, built up, only to dissipate by the evening. The drought had to break soon. People's nerves were close to shattering.

Avoiding patches of melted tar on the street, the unemployed wandered listlessly from store to store. In groups they window-shopped and chatted in loud voices. From time to time they halted and appraised a lifeless figure modelling women's lingerie. Moving on, they passed the outmoded merchandise displayed in the next window. The next display of imported foods held their interest. They pressed their faces and hands against the shop window and left greasy smudges over the plate glass. Unable to afford the goods, they strolled past the art gallery and turned the corner.

Mrs Betsy Montecland halted to catch her breath. She had dressed in a hurry, for her clothing was rumpled and her hat sat askew over her crimped curls. Her stockings had become twisted about her ankles. Gripping a large tote bag, she entered the gallery.

'You have heard the news, what a shame,' she panted. 'My bridge girls had just left when Rona Bentwood phoned, I

139

must tell them in the little shop next door. I'm sure you were the first to know. Such a dear person and who would have thought it. All these years and no one had any idea.'

Standing behind her counter, Marion glared at the woman with contempt. 'I'm not into gossip or petty chatter.'

Betsy ignored the interruption. 'Fancy that doctor not knowing until it was too late, and he studied tropical diseases all these years. I knew it. I knew that something was wrong. Imagine that he was not there when she collapsed. Too busy with his paintings and talking with shopkeepers. It's almost over for her, at death's door she is. Oh dear, what a shame, children and all.'

'All over for whom?' Marion peered at the blathering woman. 'What are you talking about?'

'So you haven't heard, my goodness. I would have thought you . . .'

'All over for whom, tell me, Betsy? Who's ill?' Marion shouted as she came around the counter.

'Hattie Auston-Jones. She's dying, collapsed late yesterday afternoon. William was away somewhere. Wonder what he was up to. It's the bilharzia they tell me. Infected Hattie years ago . . .'

'William! Poor indecisive William. He'll need someone at his side. What an opportunity for me to be there.'

'What are you mumbling about and what are you doing? Let go of me.' Betsy yelled as Marion pushed her out the door.

'Well, I never – such dreadful manners,' the old woman mouthed behind the glass door as she watched Marion run into her office to grab her purse.

'I'll tell my bridge girls, tell them how rude you are.' She vowed and toddled on her way to the shop next door.

Marion locked the gallery and dashed for her car. Horns blared, brakes screeched as she backed the car out of the slot and into the street. Disregarding the speed limit, she rushed to the hospital.

'Mrs Auston-Jones, what ward is she in?' Marion asked at the reception desk.

140

'Twenty-two second floor. Doctor's orders, only family allowed,' answered the nurse.

Marion mumbled hastily. 'Thank you,' and walked to the elevator. The nurse hurried around her desk brandishing a paper file in front of Marion. 'Only the family may visit her, doctor's orders.'

She tried to bar the passage. Marion gave her a look of contempt, sidestepped the woman and entered the elevator. Quietly the doors closed, shutting off the nurse's protests. Normally, Marion had no patience with suffering. Sorrow, Marion felt, was an ingredient that thickened the odour of antiseptic in the waiting-rooms and the corridors. Passages in the hospitals absorbed the hope and despair of patients and their loved ones.

The lift doors clanged open on the second floor. Voices came from a small waiting-room next to a private ward. Without a second thought, Marion went in. The waiting-room, furnished with four upholstered armchairs and a narrow settee, aimed at cheerfulness. Neatly placed on a low table were several glossy magazines.

Seth sat on one of the chairs. He babbled as he rubbed his hands up and down his knees as if demented. His red beard emphasised the grey in his complexion.

'It's my fault,' he said to no one particular. He glared around him as if to challenge anyone who might dispute his statement. 'I had to mind her. Ma told me, but I let her play in the stagnant water. She loved water lilies. It's my fault. The river came down. I left her . . .' Tears blinded him, 'I'm to blame, it's my fault. I want to tell her.'

Andy Anderson stood over Seth, massaging the big man's shoulders. 'Hang on old chap. It's not your fault. This is a hard country to survive in. You did all you could. Hattie loves and admires you.'

Mrs Anderson sat on the couch with her arms around Jack and Emma. Unable to comprehend the situation, the children watched their father holding onto Dr Hasling's lapels.

'Do something! Help her. Please,' William implored.

141

Toss went over to William's side and pried fingers loose from the jacket and firmly forced him back.

The doctor pleaded, wanting William to understand. 'I've done all I can, please believe me. There is nothing more I can do. It's too late, if only I had known earlier. I'm so sorry.' He walked slowly from the room.

Liam rose from the couch and pulled at his father's arm. 'Dad! Dad, I want to see Mama.'

William looked down at his son as if the boy were a stranger. Liam turned to Mr Anderson. 'Please Mr Anderson, I don't understand. Why can't I go to Mother? Please let me see her.'

The elder man rubbed his chin and glanced at his wife. 'Maybe he shouldn't.'

'Come, Liam we go together,' Marion said as she stepped farther into the room. She held out her hand to Liam who hesitated, then took her hand. Together they walked into the room where his mother lay.

From the doorway he was aware of the mottled light coming through the floral curtains. The figure in the hospital bed barely made an impression under the covers. That wasn't his mother lying there, a mere shrunken form, he was in the wrong room.

What evil being would do that to her? What lethal parasite had hibernated deep within her body for years? Then, for an unknown reason, it began stealing her life away, until her body was beyond the reach of medical aid.

Hattie twisted her head at the sound of Liam's gasp. He saw her lift her arm to beckon him. Marion encouraged him forward. 'Go to your mother.'

At the bedside he looked at her pale features. The radiance was ebbing from her eyes. She called out in disjointed phrases. 'William, come my darling. Seth? Where's Seth? He made me laugh.'

Her voice grew stronger as Liam remembered it.

'Liam . . . make Jack laugh,' Hattie said desperately. 'You must make Jack laugh.'

'Yes, Mama, I promise. Please get better quickly. Mama.'

142

Hattie lay back. Her mind began to wander and the whispering became incoherent. 'Where's Emma? Care for Emma. Emma.' She closed her eyes and whispered. 'Where's little Emma?'

Marion went up to the boy. 'Your mother must rest now. Kiss her goodbye and come away.'

Hattie's cheeks were icy cold as he touched them with his soft lips. Confused and angry with himself, Liam ran out and Marion followed him to the waiting-room.

'William must be with Hattie now,' Marion whispered to Mrs Anderson. 'You, your husband and Toss remain with William and Seth. They will need your strength. I'll take the children home and gently explain to them.'

Mrs Anderson answered. 'Maybe William should tell them. The children, they are so young.'

'Look at him, do you think he is capable?'

William, slouched against the wall, spoke above Seth's rambling.

'I promised to fix the fence and the screen door, Toss. It always slammed. Hattie wants to plant more dahlias. I'll order the bulbs tomorrow. We have hundreds of them. The field by the paddocks, they'll do well there.'

Seth's muttering blended with William's voice. 'Ma told me to mind her. "Seth," she said, "mind Hattie." ' Faster and faster Seth rubbed his hand over his knees.

'We are going to visit my mother, Seth. Hattie says the children must visit their grandmother . . .'

'. . . the old Model-T Ford, she teased me about it. I loved that old car. She made me teach Oparee to drive . . .' Saliva started to dribble from Seth's lips.

'Andy, for God's sake, you and your wife take Seth home. Give him a stiff drink or a sedative. He's in a state of shock,' cried Toss. He firmly gripped William around the shoulders. 'I'll take William to Hattie and stay with him.'

Marion guided the children from the room and led them to her car. She seated them at the back.

'You saw Mother. When she's coming home?' Jack asked Liam.

143

Emma began to scream. 'I want . . .'

'Be quiet Emma, Mama is sick,' said Jack. 'What did she tell you Liam?'

'She said something about Uncle Seth making her laugh.'

Emma stopped crying. 'Tell us Liam, tell us. How did Uncle Seth make Mama laugh?'

Jack turned to Emma. 'Remember Mama told us how Uncle Seth's arms and legs went up and down trying to climb the river bank.'

Jack and Emma giggled over their private joke. Liam sat with his head lowered and with his hands on his lap. He realised his mother was dying, she would never return home. He remembered her as one who was serene and strong. She never called for anything or any one. As she lay so ill, her thoughts were for Jack.

'Make Jack laugh,' she had told Liam in her soft comforting voice. A voice who all willingly obeyed. Why had this happened? What did he do wrong? Uncertain and confused at the sudden change in his life, he wanted someone to explain it to him now. His father, he trusted his father, not Marion. Where was his father?

The sun, a fiery ball, tipped the crescent of Pioneer Hill as Marion and the children arrived at the old house. She pulled up at the front door.

'We don't go in that way. We use the side door,' said Jack.

'Never mind that now, I have to tell you something.'

Liam swung open the car door and slipped out. Pushing his way through the hedge he disappeared. Emma stared wide-eyed about her as if expecting Marion to share a joke with her. Jack looked directly at the beautiful face. It frightened him.

'I will take your mother's . . .' She got no further. Jack gave a whimper, sensing something dreadful had happened. What had she done with his mother? He couldn't understand that. What disaster had befallen them? As Liam had done, he too slammed out of the car and pushed through the hedge. He went to the toy-box on the veranda and tossed out different

144

playthings until he found Our Haggerty. Hugging the bear he sat on the top step and stared blindly at his feet.

Emma began yelling louder and stamping her feet. 'I want my mummy, I want my mummy.'

Marion grabbed her hand and together they walked down the path. Newly planted seedlings and the dark earth smelled fresh. Marion knelt beside the child and spoke earnestly. Gradually Emma stopped her yelling and ran to an old tyre suspended from the jacaranda. The child flopped like a rag doll over the tyre, her hair almost touching the ground. She rocked slowly, back and forth.

Marion stepped onto the veranda as the screen door opened. Jourbor backed out carrying a loaded tray which he put on the table. He went to Jack and touched him on the shoulder. The boy rose and went to his chair. Jourbor jumped off the veranda to search for Liam. Minutes later they returned and Liam went to sit next to Jack. Next the servant fetched Emma from the swing. He carried her under his arm while she kicked and giggled. He sat Emma at the table and took a damp facecloth from his apron pocket. She ducked away from him.

'Augh!' Jourbor's voice was deep and guttural. It was the only word Marion would ever hear him utter. His brown hand engulfed Emma's little face as he wiped it with the face-cloth. She wriggled her nose and pouted her lips when he gave her face a final rub with the hand-towel. Taking the face-cloth from Jourbor, Liam gave his hands a perfunctory wipe. Jack sat quietly staring at the teapot.

Jourbor placed a plate of bread and butter spread with gooseberry jam on the table. From a blue teapot with a chipped lid he poured tea into coloured mugs. Jack's brown mug reminded Marion of the colour in Hattie's hair. Hattie at the cocktail party with her hair curling around her features. That was the first time she had seen Hattie. And today was the last, when Hattie lay dying.

While the children ate, Marion strolled into the house. This was the opportunity to value William's work. Maybe the pictures were just pretty as Betsy had described them and

145

were of no value. She passed the kitchen, went down the second passage and glanced into the dining-room. The polished table reflected a silver bowl of white daisies. To the left, the sideboard held a full service of crockery and silver plateware. Persian rugs scattered on the parquet floor contrasted against the rich mahogany furniture. Not a painting was to be seen on any of the walls.

Double doors opened into the first lounge and the morning room lay beyond. The smaller room to the left contained easy chairs and couches placed around the large fireplace. On the coffee table a box of dominoes lay open. Velvet curtains hung from ceiling to floor, subduing the afternoon's sunlight. The walls were void of all pictures or paintings. Marion retraced her steps and noticed the narrow room under the staircase.

What was hidden in that room? She went forward and placed her hand on the brass doorhandle. Jourbor appeared suddenly and came swiftly up the passage. He stopped and glared at her. The markings across his temples swelled, his stance was forbidding. Marion let go of the handle.

'The bwana will be here soon,' she said pushing past him. She walked quickly down the passage and banged the screen door behind her. Liam's chair was empty. Emma's giggles caught Marion's attention, she was splashing her hands in spilled tea. Marion grimaced and went forward. Jack sat on the first step. A slice of bread hung from his hand. Gooseberry jam dripped at his feet. The Haggerty bear held tight against him. He gave Marion a cold stare as she looked down at him. Frustrated and annoyed, Marion stamped on the second step. It was the same broken step which each member of the household had learned to avoid. William had promised to repair it on the day he had proposed to Hattie.

'Oh damn! I've twisted my ankle,' Marion howled and, grabbing the ivy-covered handrail for support, she felt something squish under her hand. Pulling her hand back, she saw a squashed chameleon stuck to her fingers. Its bulbous eyes stared at her, the long sticky tongue drooped over her wrist. A thin stream of green faeces erupted from its anus in a

146

perfect curve. The revolting mess landed on her skirt. Marion dropped the vile creature. Bile filled her mouth. She hobbled through the gap in the hedge and heaved against the side of the car.

Chapter 16

The mourners gathered around the grave. Friends hidden behind dark glasses wept silently. Liam blinked his eyes at the strangeness of it all. Where did all these people come from? Why were they pressing so close?

'Where's Mama?' Jack's voice pleaded for an answer. 'Please Liam, where's Mama?' The younger boy tugged on Liam's coat.

Emma, standing between William and Jack, pulled a grubby glove from her hand, the other glove was discarded on the path. She waved the glove at Hattie's coffin. A single dahlia, its dark foliage reflected in polished oak, lay on the casket. Wreaths, each with cards of condolence attached to the greenery, were laid close by.

'She's in that box with the pretty flower on it,' Emma explained to her brother. 'They are going to put her in the hole. We'll cover the box with sand. It's like a game of hide-and-seek.'

Who had explained the proceedings of a funeral to Emma? She was too little to understand. Liam heard Emma's voice as a jumble of words that intruded on the singsong voice of the parson.

This was not the right kind of day for a funeral. The first rains of the wet season had washed the paths and the earth smelled fresh and rich. The time of renewed life, verdant fields and stilled air. White and yellow butterflies fluttered in a protective mass over a patch of damp ground.

What am I doing here, Liam wondered. This is all so

weird, it's not real at all. Now is the time when Mama serves tea and cake on the veranda. He usually rode Frith up to the house at teatime. With reins firmly in his hands, he controlled the pony as it cantered up the drive. Jack usually perched on his favourite branch of the jacaranda reading his book. Occasionally, he licked at the traces of chocolate cake around his mouth. Emma, as usual, played near the frog pond with the mud dripping down her clothes. Liam could hear his father say, 'Am I expected to eat Emma's mud pies?' Liam heard again Mama's laughing reply. 'Of course.'

Yet here he stood in this unreal setting. Women behind him sniffed into handkerchiefs and men wiped their eyes. He, Liam, couldn't cry. Had he not promised his mother he would make Jack laugh.

A string of cars like a coloured centipede, had trailed them from the cathedral. On rubber legs the disjointed body bobbed and swayed. Arriving at the cemetery, passengers emerged from their cars. They moved slowly as black beetles crawl from under rocks. Up the path they shuffled behind the pall-bearers, all so deathly quiet. In the middle of the graveyard the column divided to pass the msasa tree. The old tree protected a single grave, a pioneer's resting place. The cemetery spread over and down the hillside.

Liam knew everything about dying. All eleven-year-old boys knew how a person died. Jack read about death in his cowboy books.

They die with their arms straight out and they fall flat on their faces.

No one dies quietly in their beds. Nor do mothers tell you to make your brother laugh or call for their children. Dull rainy days are for funerals. Graves are all dark, soggy and deep. No, decided Liam, the day was too cheerful for a funeral.

He shrugged in his new suit. Today he didn't object to wearing it. He wore it in retribution for past sins. Jack didn't mind dressing up, in fact he liked being smart. Marion had bought these new clothes for all of them. William wore his new suit and Emma, her new dress. It was a dainty dark

150

print with a lace collar. To complete the ensemble Emma wore tiny white gloves and a straw hat. Marion had refused to let her wear her cotton bonnet.

'You're a big girl now. Only babies wear bonnets,' Marion told the child. 'Your father will be proud of you.'

'Liam and Jack will laugh at me,' pouted the child.

Marion had allayed Emma's objections firmly. The clothes cost a lot of money.

The preacher at the head of the grave intoned a prayer. Liam lifted his head to watch two little clouds playing tag in the big blue sky. A hand gripped his shoulder. Twisting around he met Marion's reproachful glance. She wore her ivory linen ensemble with modesty and decorum. The wide-brimmed hat protected her olive complexion and shaded her exquisite green eyes.

Liam had a picture of an Egyptian queen in his history book. Marion looked like one. A real queen with a curved body and long legs. Those green eyes, which either flashed or narrowed into pinpoints, frightened him. She told the children to call her Marion, not Mrs Russell or Auntie Marion, just Marion. Jack refused to speak to her, let alone call her anything. Emma either cried for her mother or flung her sticky hands and arms around Marion's neck.

Marion was funny, too. She offered them money to search for hidden keys. Why she wanted keys for the bedroom cupboards, she didn't say. Bribes were unnecessary. He always felt proud to obey his mother. His reward was a gentle smile or a word of praise. That made him feel proud. When Marion approached Jack, he stuck his tongue out at her.

Liam turned his attention to his father standing by the grave. Why did he slouch so and shake his head? What dreadful thought was he trying to dispel?

'Where's Mama?' Jack tugged persistently on Liam's coat.

'I told you in there,' said Emma twisting around to face Marion. 'When it gets dark, Mama will climb out, fly way up to heaven and be a star. Won't she, Marion?'

Liam heard his father say, 'Hush, Emma.' His voice was

151

dry as the leaves that the wind scratched against the tomb-stones.

Jack turned from the burial service. Marion held out her hand to the boy but he shrank from the red lacquered finger-nails. He ran blindly, dodging the graves until he reached the msasa tree. He held his face against the trunk, his curly hair blending with the hard bark.

William lifted Emma and pressed her head to his shoulder. Her straw hat slipped and fell to the ground.

'Hush,' he repeated, 'we will go home soon.'

Liam knew Marion loathed dust or traces of grime, saying it led to poverty. That's why she grimaced as Emma's shoes muddied William's new suit.

The parson closed his prayer-book, offered his condolences and started down the path.

'Come, we'll find Jack and go home now.' William set Emma down and took her hand.

Marion put her hand on Liam's shoulder. 'We'll go with your father.'

He pulled away and went ahead to walk beside his sister.

'Let me drive you home,' suggested Andy Anderson when they reached the car.

William held the door open for Marion and shook his head. 'It's all right Marion is with me, I'll manage.'

Emma squeezed past her father and pulled on Marion's skirt. 'I want to sit in front with you.'

'No. Come now Emma, be a good girl and get in the back with your brothers.'

'No,' screamed Emma. 'I always sit with my Mama. I want Mama. I don't want her in that box.'

The child began to wail. William gave Marion a wan smile and lifted the child. 'Let her sit on your lap.'

They drove slowly from the cemetery. From the car's window Liam watched the mourners climbing into their vehicles. They went past the abandoned construction sites. Fingers of reinforced concrete pointed accusingly at the sky.

'The world is so empty now,' Liam said to Jack, 'don't you think so?'

152

Jack nodded. He was staring at Emma's sweaty hand on Marion's ivory linen skirt. Liam saw the expression of disgust come over Marion's face as she looked down at the sleeping child. At the house William lifted Emma from Marion's lap. 'I'll take her to her bedroom.'

'We want to go to the paddocks. May we, Dad, me and Jack?' Liam entreated.

'Ah, I don't know . . . yes I suppose so.'

'William, your friends will be arriving shortly.' Marion spoke with the authority of a chosen leader. 'The boys are wearing their new clothes.'

William responded. '. . . better stay . . . for a while.' Carrying Emma, he went into the house.

Marion held out her hand to Jack. 'Come, let's go and see what Jourbor has made.' Again the boy ignored her outstretched hand and ran up the steps. Not knowing what to do, Liam followed Marion into the kitchen. Jourbor stood staring out the window, ignoring their entrance.

'Take the drinks and sandwiches into the lounge, Jourbor,' commanded Marion. He remained motionless, still as a block of ebony, his expression inscrutable. Liam saw Marion's eyes narrow, her jaw muscles contract.

'I spoke to you Jourbor. Your mistress has died, there's nothing we can do to bring her back. Wear a clean apron.'

The servant remained stationary.

'Now there's work to be done. The bwana's friends are coming. Hurry.' She moved to the counter. 'This teapot has a chipped lid.'

Jourbor continued to stare out the window.

'Get the other teapot, the silver one, in the dining-room. Use that.'

Liam pressed himself against the wall as Marion stamped out of the kitchen and then followed her.

The first mourners had arrived. Liam saw William at the liquor cabinet filling a glass of whisky.

'You shouldn't be drinking,' said Marion, 'you have taken medication. The Bentwoods are here.'

William shrugged and lifted his glass. She went forward.

153

Someone had to greet and take care of the sympathetic gathering. They came through the front door into the first lounge, wearing sad faces and murmuring condolences. Whispered words of sympathy. Arm touching, back rubbing, back patting. Kissing, hugging. Lamenting and commiserating.

Liam and Jack sat cramped together on the couch like two cells in a sea of grey and black plasma that contracted and expanded around them. Oily hands stretched out to slick down their hair. Liam dodged one hot wet hand that reached out, only to feel other thick fingers pulling at his hair.

Liam pointed towards the open door as a black sedan drew up. 'Look, Jack, that car has flags on the hood. Someone important has arrived.'

A chauffeur briskly stepped out, opened the rear door and he leaned forward to help an elderly man. The gentleman, stooped and whiskered, entered the house. He moved quickly through the gathering and touched William on the shoulder for a moment. William acknowledged the commiseration with a nod. On his way out, the visitor stopped in front of the two little boys. He shook his head sadly then hurried back to his car.

Marion overhearing the talk, trembled as she stood by William's side.

'She was such a dear.'

'Thank you for coming.'

'Yes. William's holding up.'

'Children are brave.'

Whispers.

'Marion's been wonderful. Isaac is very friendly with her.'

'Another cup, Betsy?'

Mrs Betsy Montecland gripped the cup in a bony hand. Her diamond-ringed finger supported a cucumber sandwich on the saucer.

'I say, Charlie, she's not waiting.' Betsy pointed at Marion. 'She's been after him for weeks. First she was all over him in the art gallery and now over his house and children.' Betsy popped the morsel of bread behind her big teeth.

'Poor Hattie. Body not yet cold,' someone said.

154

'I wonder where all his paintings are?' said Charlie Monte-cland, looking around.

'Yes. I wonder what has happened to the pretty picture of butterflies and little animals. Hattie showed it to me once, poor dear. Well, we better get going.'

In twos and threes the sympathisers left. Mourners came forward to shake hands. There was pressing of cheeks, bidding of farewells, and thank you's for coming.

Eventually all the guests left. Marion and William were alone. Liam heard Marion mumbling an apology to his father.

'I'm sorry about what Emma said at the funeral. I tried to make it easy for her, to pacify her. She misunderstood my explanation.'

William slowly focused his eyes on her, not seeing her. She found it difficult to hold his gaze.

'The old teapot, the one with the chipped lid. It makes better tea. Where is it?'

Liam ran from the room. It was all so confusing. His father's concern over a teapot. Marion making excuses and being rude to Jourbor. Liam threw his new jacket, shoes and tie into the dust and jumped onto his cycle. Jack sat on the step squeezing Our Haggerty to his shoulder, his thumb stuck in his mouth. A wet patch covered the front of his pants.

Round and round the tree Liam cycled. Finally, he halted and balanced himself against the trunk. If only he could cry, it might help. A pain pulled inside him, in a place that was impossible to touch. Maybe tears would ease the ache, but he couldn't cry. Everything around him made him feel so strange.

'I warned you Marion.' Voices came to Liam from the garage. Quietly, he cycled closer and looked in. Rona Bentwood pointed a finger at Marion. 'There's talk. You heard them talking in there.'

'What do you mean?'

'Isaac visiting you in hospital.'

'He brought me some flowers from my staff. He's thoughtful. Why the other day he warned me about his sister, said she's a thief. She wants Hattie's diamond clasp. Isaac suggested I find it and keep it safe. Who is spreading the malicious gossip?'

'Maybe Isaac is well-meaning, but town criers like Betsy perpetuate and exaggerate any morsel of gossip.'

Rona Bentwood straightened her hat. Liam wondered why she was not wearing her cardigan. She looked strange without it.

'And now you are all over William,' Rona went on. 'You heard them, linking your name to Isaac's and now William's. If your reputation is immaterial to you, at least don't start a racial conflict. Think my words over carefully, before you do anything.'

Through tight lips Marion said, 'I'll take your advice and squash all the scandal. When the children are asleep, I'll go to my own place.'

'That'll be best for all.' Rona stumbled out of the garage to her car.

'I wonder what she is thinking about,' Liam asked himself as Marion walked slowly back to the house. He began circling the tree again and again.

Dressed in slacks and sweater Marion tapped her foot against the bedside table in the guest room. A cigarette burned in her fingers. In the next room the children slept and downstairs William lay in a deep sedated sleep on the couch.

Rona is right, she thought. I can't afford a scandal but how can I get control of William and his wealth. Certainly not through his sons, they are impossible to manipulate. There must be some way, I'm sure the answer lies in this house. She stamped out the cigarette in the ashtray and with a look of disgust, she threw the ashtray into the wastepaper basket.

Charlie Montecland's voice came back to her. 'Where were all the paintings?'

Marion opened the bedroom door and peeped out, no one

156

was in sight. Carrying her suitcase, she went down the stairs and stopped in front of the narrow door. It opened at her touch. From a dark corner a pair of ghostly eyes glowed at her. She stepped back, petrified. The door slammed closed and the darkness became absolute. Cowering from fright, hands in front of her face, she felt terror rising within her.

'Dear God in Heaven what is staring at me?' she whispered. Gradually light infiltrated the blackness. She turned her head from those burning eyes. Another pair stared at her. Twisting around she looked left. Other eyes peered down.

Eyes, hundreds of eyes followed her movements. Again she twisted. More eyes, green, blue, orange eyes. Dead eyes, mocking eyes. Some suspended, some at her feet, all waiting. Fifty pairs of eyes in a row stared at her. Her body stiffened and her mouth went dry. Slowly, she raised her hand and found the light switch. In the artificial light the eyes that petrified her shone in a blaze of colour and form. William's twelve paintings filled the room. These were his gifts to Hattie, one for each year of their marriage. She gasped at the beauty of the spectacle around her.

Most of the work depicted some form of wildlife. All the details of each animal were authentically portrayed. The impala's liquid eyes, its delicate brown and white body poised. False eyes on butterfly's wings so lifelike yet, as they were meant to be, false. Crafty eyes in the winsome faces of the monkeys that hung from the msasa trees. A herd of fifty buffalo stood in a line, their eyes expressing curiosity. The fixed look of the giraffe mocked her.

He had painted birds in flight and birds with their young. He had captured the colouring of the lilac-breasted roller and the shape of the nightjar's cruel beak. A picture of an owl in the moonlight held her attention. A wash over the work added a mystic quality. In the corner of the picture a little smiling green frog peeped from a pool of water. It was out of context, probably added sometime later. Was it a message, or a reminder?

Marion stood there in a trance. This was the talent she had been searching for. To kill such genius through depression or

157

deaden the mind with alcohol and drugs would be sacrilegious. Encouragement and motivation, that's what he needed and she would give him both. What a fortune she would make but how with all the scandal surrounding her? She must wait for the right moment.

Quietly, she let herself out of the room. A pair of white living eyes with deep brown pupils watched her emerge from the room. Jourbor followed her down the passage and out of the house.

Chapter 17

Isaac glanced discreetly to the right and left, before he slipped into the gallery.

'Where's Marion?' Isaac ordered as he placed a crudely wrapped parcel on the counter. 'Call her, I'm in a hurry.'

'Isaac's here on business,' the assistant told Marion in the office.

'Thanks. I'll come out while you take your tea break.'

Alone with Marion in the gallery, Isaac gave up all pretence of conducting business.

'Here,' he said and placed the parcel into Marion's hands. 'Look at this.'

Surprised at the weight of the small package, she quickly discarded the brown paper and uncovered a small effigy. The cold face etched in the ivory reminded her of a Middle Eastern death mask. Its features, high cheekbones and pouting lips were similar to those of the man who stood before her. Pivoting the statuette to the light, she sighed and placed it on the counter.

'Unfortunately I can't afford this unique piece,' Marion said. 'It's really delightful. The artist deserves a fair price for it, and he probably needs the money to feed his family.'

In his usual manner Isaac flicked his hand, dismissing the plight of the artist. He leaned over the counter and caught her arm. 'How much progress are you making with William?'

'None.'

'Rubbish. You are not fooling me,' sneered Isaac. 'We are two of a kind. Smart enough to know what we want. I

159

want his patriotism and you'll want something more than his money one day. Probably it will be revenge. Don't look so annoyed, I admire you. I'll keep our relationship under covers if you can get William to join my political party.'

Marion met his challenge. She stared directly at him.

'So that's what you have been angling for. Now you're blackmailing me. Just remember your social position is as precarious as mine; ridicule will discredit both of us. Besides I can't influence William.'

Isaac eased her words with a laugh. 'You're smart. Yes, we both must be careful. Please understand I need you and, I promise you, one day together we'll lead the nation.' Isaac stood up. The charming smile on his lips belied the malice in his eyes. 'You're right, talk and scandal will ruin our chances. When I'm the president, you'll redecorate Government House for me. I'll want one of Auston-Jones's paintings hung there. You must get one for me.'

'How could I?'

'Oh, you will, with your talents you'll find a way.'

Isaac thrust the statue into her hand. As quietly as he had entered the gallery, he slipped out.

The oppressive heat and muggy nights sapped Marion's strength. She awoke each morning feeling depressed and irritable and the very notion of failure intensified her temper. Her business teetered on the edge of bankruptcy. It was collapsing partly because the citizens were preparing to migrate. For them the luxury of having artifacts had become superfluous. The tourist trade dwindled as pleasure seekers looked elsewhere for entertainment. Furthermore, her schemes to ensnare William and, ultimately, to control his wealth had eluded her. Too many obstacles stood between them – family, friends and malicious gossip.

The phone rang, a strident ring that jarred her thoughts and aggravated her further. No doubt it was another demand to settle an outstanding account.

'Answer it,' she abruptly commanded her assistant who had just entered the gallery.

'It's for you,' said the assistant and handed her the receiver.

160

Marion listened, her eyes widened. A smile spread over her face.

'. . . I admit maybe I did overreact.' Rona was apologising. 'Andy Anderson and I are at our wits end. We think you're the only person who can help William. God knows, we've tried.'

'Where is Seth?'

'I haven't seen him since the day Hattie died. He is most likely at his farm.'

'What's William doing, painting?'

'Heavens no, he lolls in bed all morning and gets drunk by four in the afternoon. He neglects the children and scolds them. I never thought William could be so unjust, he has a cruel streak. David, you know my husband, always said . . .'

'Yes, yes I know your husband. Tell me more about William?'

Rona sniffed. 'We have pleaded with him but he is hard and unyielding.'

'Are the household servants working?' asked Marion.

'No, they congregate in their quarters, drinking, talking and neglecting their duties. Except Jourbor, he is a faithful servant. He tries to comfort the children and protect them from William's drunken bouts. Little Emma is in and out of the servants' rooms at all hours. Liam rides around the tree all day. William won't allow him near the paddocks or his pony for some unknown reason. Jack sits on the step with his thumb in his mouth, never saying a word.'

There was a long pause over the phone. Eventually Rona spoke. 'Are you still there?'

'Ah yes, Rona,' Marion answered vaguely. 'I was thinking of a plan, but it won't work if there are continuous rumours about me.'

'Don't worry, the Andersons and I will put a stop to any talk.'

'Good. Now can you get William to visit me, tell him I need him. Stress the word *need*, that will get him to come.'

'Sure, I'll see him this afternoon.'

Marion rang off, thought awhile then drew out her note-

161

book and listed William's closest and most influential friends, including the ambassador. The mourners had been in awe of HE. They all stood up when he arrived at Hattie's wake, Marion recalled. They stood at attention as he entered the room and respectfully let him pass. Obviously His Excellency held William in high regard if he took the time to attend the wake.

Marion held out her hand and without looking at her assistant said, 'Pass me the phone directory.'

She quickly flicked her fingers through the dog-eared pages as she searched for a phone number. A crafty smile touched her lips as she lifted the phone, dialled and spoke briefly. The assistant looked over her shoulder and saw the long red fingernails impatiently tapping on the glass counter. Marion waited. Two minutes later she spoke again.

'I'm Marion Russell. Thank you for giving me a few moments of your time, sir,' Marion began. 'It's about William Auston-Jones, I need your help . . .'

The ambassador, on the other end of the line, recalled the beautiful woman standing at William's side after Hattie's funeral. He remembered the remarks made by the guests. 'Can't wait to get him.'

'Understand this, Mrs Russell,' he interrupted, 'neither I nor my staff will aid you in any schemes which will compromise William's family or his reputation.'

'Your Excellency, I have never needed an ambassador or anyone else's aid to fuck any man,' answered Marion.

'Very well, Mrs Russell, I think we understand one another.'

'My concern is for William's welfare and his children. They need help.'

'What do you suggest?'

'Give him a reason to paint once more. Encourage him to paint a picture in Hattie's memory. That may help him work through his grief.'

'How could I inspire him?'

Marion outlined her plan.

'Very well,' His Excellency agreed. 'I shall give your

162

suggestions my serious consideration. Then I'll speak with the Andersons and the Bentwoods.'

Two days later William swung his car into Marion's driveway. Jamming on the brakes, he brought it to a halt in a flurry of dust and gravel. After the dust settled, he climbed unsteadily from the car and staggered along the path. Half way to the door, he stopped to take a drink from the bottle in his hand.

After a loud belch he wiped his mouth and continued his trip up the path. Eyeing his bare chest he shook his head. Thoughts of visiting a lady with an opened shirt were bad manners. Holding the first button between finger and thumb, he tried to locate the corresponding hole. The project became too difficult with one hand so he bent down cautiously and set the whisky bottle on the gravel. Tottering unsteadily, he straightened up.

After a concentrated effort, he finally buttoned his shirt. With an irrational grin he began tucking the ends of the shirt into his creased jeans. The effort became too much so he picked up his bottle, took another long pull and weaved his way to the house. At the door he lifted the bottle and rapped it against the wood. He waited for a moment as if to gather strength before he banged a second time.

Not hearing Marion's yell, 'Hold that racket,' from inside, William raised the bottle above his head. This time, determined to smash it, he threw his body forward as the door flew open. Unable to control his momentum, he toppled through the doorway and crashed onto a chair.

Marion screamed in panic. 'Get out you, vagrant!'

William, twisted around and leered sarcastically at her. 'Well me darlin', here I am, all yours at last. Old Rona said you needed me. Can't wait any more, can you? Desperate aren't you. Are ya . . . goin' to ask me to sit, or go straight to bed? Let's play. I always want to play . . .'

Burping again he came for her, his bloodshot eyes half-closed. Marion sidestepped him. 'You're drunk, you yellow spineless cur.'

'Not quite drunk, me darlin', only half drunk. I drove here

163

didn't I? Yes, you're so right. I've always been spineless, can't make up my mind what I want.'

'Get out!'

As if he were completely sober, William referred to his past. 'Never could make up my mind, didn't have to. At school they did it for me. In the army, they ordered me to kill. I killed lots of people . . . didn't want to kill them, I love people. I wanted to paint your portrait.'

'You lie, you wanted to screw me but you hadn't the guts to try. You'll regret fooling with me. I'll make you pay.'

'Sure I'll pay,' he said as drink clouded his mind. 'How much does a prostitute like you charge? Everything a man owns and his reputation. Or do you work for nothing?'

Marion went cold with anger. 'You bloody high and mighty bastard. Nobody calls me a prostitute. You'll pay for your remarks. I'll strip you of everything you have. Get out!'

'You wanted to get me alone. For months you wanted, what's the genteel word for fuck, eh? Fornicate! That's it . . .' William swayed and burped. 'Me, the cream of society will fornicate with you, a bitch in heat. Let's have a drink first. Got the bottle, see.' William staggered to the couch and pulled at his shirt. 'Wait, le' me take my clothes off. Or do you want to unzip me.'

'Get out!'

'Come on, Marion, since you first met me, you wanted to get into my pants, fluttering your eyelashes and wiggling your fanny at me.' William gave a mirthless laugh. 'Old Charlie Montecland enjoyed watching you. Remember how you lured me into your house. Now that was very clever of you. Stage all neatly set, imported tulips, an' all. Did you have the drinks ready? Were the bedclothes turned down?'

Marion blushed, for he spoke the truth. 'Degenerate that you are, at least I'm honest about it. You, with your hands in your pockets and fingering your balls. Slinking into my gallery with your "like to feel my subject" approach.'

Marion came further into the room, stood by the window. She sneered at William, her features registering the loathing she felt. 'You hadn't the guts to come to my bed. You sniffed

164

around like a cur with its tail between its legs. Used your daughter as a chaperone, some lover boy.'

'What a crop of ... I'll show you.' He staggered up to her. 'Come on my girl, what's stopping you. Hattie's cold in her grave now.'

Marion spat at him with loathing. 'For Christ's sake William, sober up. Let Hattie rest in peace.'

'Hattie to rest in ... p ... peace,' he snorted, 'what a laugh that is. You wouldn't let her alone. Wanted her out of the way, so you could take her place.' He made a grab at her. 'Come on, she can't stop you now.'

Marion lifted a jug of water and threw the contents over his face. Startled, he halted in his tracks. He dropped onto the couch, wiping the water from his face with his hands.

She looked down at him. If he had any self-respect, he'd get up and slap her. William remained on the couch, shivering and disoriented.

She sniggered hideously. 'You're a wimp.'

Wimp, wimp. A kite-faced wimp. These words echoed through William's memory. His father's ridicule resounded down the years. All the insults cleared the drunken vapours from his mind. His humiliation was unbearable. Jumping up from the couch and raising the whisky bottle above his head, he lunged at her.

Marion stood her ground. 'Go on, you cowardly swine, look at yourself in the mirror before you hit me.'

William swung around and saw his reflection. He saw his unshaven face, unwashed hair and bloodshot eyes, and his soiled clothes horrified him. He smashed the bottle against the mirror. Glass splinters shattered over the carpet and rivulets of liquor trickled down the wall.

'You haven't the guts to hit me. You're a disgrace to your forefathers, the supposed-to-be leaders in society,' Marion continued insulting him. 'What did the old sister in the hospital tell me? You were symbolic of the nation. You symbolize nothing but a wimp. Safe, you hide in your house beyond the trees. Rolling in luxury or cringing in a stupor of alcohol. Your children, do you know what's happening to them?'

165

'What am *I* doing to them? Remember what *you* told them. Said that their mother's in a box and we planted her. You enjoyed frightening a little girl and horrifying small boys. Is that your idea of comfort and sympathy?'

Marion bit her lip, she had been very cruel. He now had control of the situation. Confessions made her vulnerable but she had to apologise.

'I'm sorry, William, so deeply sorry. It was the wrong way to pacify Emma but that's the only way I knew. Rona said . . .' Marion hesitated, unwilling to make excuses.

'Bitch,' he shouted. 'Is this another one of your schemes? Buttering up Rona to come to spy on me, eh. Rona, the keeper of the gospel; always twitching at her clothing. Ha! Her idea of charity is to hand out goodwill like a bloody fairy godmother. Doing you a pretty favour, was she?'

Marion gripped the back of the chair, the humiliation sent her thoughts racing. He had missed his chance. Through his children she'd continue to belittle him.

'You egotistic swine, you think only of yourself. Look at your children, forgotten and lonely. Liam riding in an endless circle, no one to hold him. Jack just sits on the top step wetting his pants . . .'

William whispered. 'She always sat there, watching the sunset. Her eyes were so serene. Hattie, I must not let you down, I'll care for our children and for their future.'

'. . . Hugging that teddy bear, day after day not saying anything, waiting for his mother's return.' Marion went closer to him, her eyes, two green points of light. In a fiendishly low voice she said. 'Emma. Where's Emma?' Her wet tongue slipped in and out of her mouth as if checking the tension. 'Those were Hattie's last words, "where's Emma?" I tell you where she is. In the backyard and grubbing about in her nanny's room. Jourbor is in charge now and feeding the children on bread and that reeking jam. There's no telling what he might do to Hattie's children.'

William brushed past Marion to the door. With his back to her he murmured. 'Hattie? Oh Hattie I must be strong for you. How can I? What must I do?'

166

'Why don't you think of others, Seth and your friends? They also loved and now miss Hattie. They haven't the luxury of sitting and wailing or of drinking themselves into oblivion. For Hattie's sake, protect what she loved.'

'What Hattie loved?' he repeated. 'Hattie loved her children and the wildlife around her, and this country. She heard the heartbeat of the land. Through her eyes I saw beauty around me. I miss her and the children want her home. What can I do to ease the pain that hurts so deep inside me? Is there any way to help me?'

'Yes there is,' she told him.

'What, tell me?'

'Paint a picture for her, a special one in her memory. Present it to the people. It will be a token of your faith in the nation. Let the world see it.'

Head held high and shoulders back, William left the house. No one saw the tears flowing down his face or knew of the pain in his heart.

The morning was clear and fresh when William called the children to him. He held Emma close and explained as tenderly as he could why Hattie had left them. Jack, holding Our Haggerty, stood in front of his father, staring him down.

'It is wrong to blame ourselves.' William met Jack's accusing stare. 'Your mother didn't die because we did something bad. She became very ill and was in pain.'

'Is she coming back?' asked Jack.

This was the saddest question William ever answered. He looked across to the garden. The dahlias were in full bloom.

'No,' he answered softly. 'Your mama is at rest now and we must go on living. In time we must try to be happy. That's what we must do.'

Jack nodded and Liam shifted from his side. Smoothing Emma's hair, William entreated, 'I need you to help me. I must paint one more picture for your mother. When I have finished it, I'll take you to visit your grandmother. She lives by the sea.'

Gradually William established a daily routine. The

167

children were kept occupied and cared for while he painted, managed his estate and financial affairs. At bedtime he took a bottle of whisky to his room. The liquor eased his heartache.

Chapter 18

'What is wrong with this phone? That's a dreadful crackling.' Marion shook the handset. 'That's better. How's William coping?'

Rona, her voice somewhat distorted, answered. 'He is a changed man, full of confidence. I don't know what you said to him or what happened. It seems as if the tragedy of Hattie's death has made him aware of the future. He has improved his estate, enlarging the stables and Liam is allowed to ride his pony. The children are into a routine and they're getting regular wholesome meals.'

Marion grimaced, she wanted to know if William was working. The children's activities were no concern of hers. She asked blatantly. 'Is he painting?'

'I can't say, I haven't seen any canvasses about. Why don't you visit him? He'll be encouraged if he had a colleague to chat to.'

'That's a good idea. I'll go out tomorrow morning. Thanks Rona.' Marion replaced the receiver.

Beyond the line of trees, silhouetted against the pale blue sky, a broad-shouldered figure moved slowly. In his arms he held a small bundle of kindling. Jourbor felt ashamed. Too often these days, now that Hattie had gone, he neglected his duties and let the fire die out. No one needed continuous hot water in the kitchen. The staff used the hot water from the bathroom now. Where that supply of hot water came from, Jourbor did not care. He bent down to pick up another twig.

Marion stopped the car and glanced at the road before

169

her. The skirmish with Liam and his pony happened about here. Which tree, she wondered idly, had her car crunched into? William had helped her then. Was it a decade ago? No it was only six months past. Then she had confidence in her abilities to snare William and play along with Isaac. Scheming, planning and making events happen had all been a game to her. Not now; the situation was deadly serious. What kind of reception awaited her beyond the trees? Her future depended on it.

'Jourbor,' she called, but he ignored her and continued to collect his firewood. Marion trembled – that man gave her the creeps.

She inched the car forward and called out again. 'I said Jourbor, is your master in?'

Without a sign that he had heard her, Jourbor when on his way. Marion accelerated and drove to the house.

'There's the Jag, so William might be home,' Marion muttered as she parked in front of the open garage. Although bright flowers filled the garden, the place looked desolate and unused. Dust and dried leaves drifted over the veranda. William's old patched sweater lay in shreds on the divan. The wool made a cosy nest for a family of field mice. An assortment of tools covered the lid of the toy-box. There was no evidence of an artist's activity. Marion thought she heard quiet voices calling but it was only the wind blowing over the broken step.

She entered the house through the screen door. William stood at the end of the passage holding a picture at arm's length. His checked shirt showed bright against the shadows. He glanced at her briefly and said indifferently. 'Hi. How are you?'

'I'm fine thanks.' She eyed the whimsical painting which he held. 'What are you going to do with that, not selling it I hope?'

'Heavens no, I thought I would hang this one. Jack gave it the title *Funny Bugs*. The picture might cheer him. He is having a difficult time, clings to that teddy bear.'

170

'It's so hard for the children. Have you spoken to them about Hattie?'

'Yes, I have. Time will help.'

'Where are they?'

'Who . . . oh the children. The boys are at school. Emma spends most mornings with Rona. That courageous lady has taken it upon herself to keep Emma clean. It's a difficult task.'

Marion laughed and gaining confidence, hinted, 'You . . . are painting?'

'I'm trying to but I've got artist's block, if there is such an ailment. Want to see what I'm doing?'

William placed the picture against the wall. 'The front room is my studio now, this way.'

Marion trailed behind him into the first lunge. The furniture filled the end of the room and the carpet held traces of spilled paint. Together they stood in front of the easel and examined the work. Marion narrowed her eyes and stepped back for an overall view.

'It's good but lacks vitality and energy.' Avoiding William's eye she asked, 'What did Rona tell you?'

'She told me that HE is retiring shortly. He wants to present some recently formed political party with a token of goodwill before he leaves. What better than a painting done by me in Hattie's memory?'

Marion held her breath, waited.

Snap!

The paintbrush in William's hand broke into fragments.

'Christ Almighty! Why can't they leave us alone?' He threw the splinters at his feet.

'It's important to HE. Won't you help him?'

'Yes,' William answered harshly. 'I'll paint one more picture.'

Marion smiled to herself and studied the painting again. 'You need a subject which the people can relate to.'

William, with hands in his pockets slouched to the window. 'I am going to the game park tomorrow,' he said. 'During the past years I've enjoyed many days there, studying

171

the wildlife. Come with me if you wish. It's a small park. Although the safari camp is a five-hour drive from here, the turn-off into the park is close by.'

'Me! In the bush. You're mad. I can't stand all that dust and grime and horrid crawling insects.' Marion shuddered in horror. Anything that flew or crawled was an affliction to mankind. She was a city girl. The larger the city the better.

'It's time I fetched the children, call me if you change your mind.'

Marion arrived the next morning suitably clad for the outing. Protected completely with a net over her hat and face and gloves on her hands.

'Good heavens,' William exclaimed, 'why are you wearing all that clothing?'

'Either I wear this or stay at home.'

'Very well, let's get going, we must be in camp before dark.'

'We're not going in that!' exclaimed Marion seeing the jeep. 'Not an open vehicle, there's no protection. Can't we go in the Jag?'

'The roads are too rough and it uses too much petrol,' William answered. 'Hattie loved this . . . Oh what the hell! We'll take the Jag, and carry extra petrol.'

The fresh country air heartened William. At times he hummed fragments from schoolboy songs. Two miles from the entrance to the park he pulled the car off the main road.

'There is an interesting view from here,' he said. 'Look behind you. See the highway, it loops around the city. Ahead the road passes the sporting complex about a mile or two from here. On the other side of the road, by that stand of trees, is a revered site for the natives. Many years ago their indabas took place there.'

'What are indabas?'

'It means gatherings or meetings. Tribal chiefs discussed war tactics and political strategies with their subjects. In those days the chief held control of the people.'

'Do they still meet there?'

172

'I don't know if there is a legitimate chief around here. Can you see a granite rock? To the people it's consecrated ground. Only the chief is allowed to stand on it and deliver his message. Come, we better get going. We are near the gates of the park.'

Crumbling concrete blocks marked the entrance. Inside the park the road branched. Fresh blades of grass, quickened by the rains, grew in clumps around the base of the trees. A shrike, with fast-beating wings, swept down and snatched an insect. The bird disappeared as quickly as it had come.

'This place has deteriorated since I was last here. I suppose the park manager has found greener pastures,' said William.

'Why do you take this rough track? The other was better.'

'More chance of seeing game on this road. The other goes directly to the safari camp.'

William shifted gears and drove slowly along the bumpy track.

'What has happened to the game? I thought this park teemed with them,' Marion asked.

'Probably all shot out by now. The poachers use powerful rifles – there's not much chance for the animals.'

The car skidded to a stop as William braked. He leaned across her. 'Over there! Open the window.'

Marion looked doubtfully. 'Sure you want me to, I thought it was against the rules of the park.'

'Open it! There's an unusual bird.' William lifted his field-glasses. 'I can't make out what it is, probably a juvenile female weaver.'

'Who cares,' muttered Marion. She adjusted her veil securely around her face.

They drove on slowly, occasionally stopping to take photographs.

'As the daylight fades, we won't be able to see much. Let's move on to the safari camp,' William suggested.

Thirty minutes later they reached the lodge. Several thatched huts, in a semi-circle around an open dining area, formed the safari lodge. A camp-fire of blackened logs

173

burned fitfully close to a spreading monkey-bread tree. Its sausage-like fruit hung low over the fire.

'How primitive,' exclaimed Marion.

'Yes it is. There's no roof on the washroom. You must be careful of snakes, they like the rough concrete floor.'

'Let's go home.'

'Too late.' He laughed.

The caretaker of the lodge, an elderly person with bent limbs, served them supper on a rickety dinner table. As they ate, black smoke rose from the paraffin lamp and William casually swatted the flying insects as they bombarded the lamplight. Marion shivered when each carcass fell.

After supper they sat by the camp-fire, now burning brightly, and the rhythms of the night began. William slouched in his chair, a glass of whisky held lightly in his fingers. He gazed pensively at the flames. Distorted images came and went – visions of faces, fragments of laughter, expressions of amazement and moments of delight.

'Come,' he said after awhile and with apologetic smile, 'it's agony for you to stay out here.'

Together they went to the first chalet. Marion looked at the sparsely furnished room. Sleeping nets hung above two narrow cots. Fine dust covered the surface of a three-legged table that leaned against the whitewashed wall.

Marion trembled. 'How uncivilised. Why are you looking at the roof?'

'I'll hold the lamp higher. There now, can you see those tiny holes in the wood? That's where all the fine dust comes from.'

Placing the lamp on the table he went to the cot and braced his foot on the frame. 'Worms, known as borers, make these tiny holes. They eat the wood and eventually the roof falls in,' he continued as he shoved the cot against the other. 'It looks okay for now, the roof won't cave in on us tonight.'

'On us!'

William raised his eyebrows, surprised at Marion's tone of voice. 'You want to sleep with me? I owe you . . .'

174

'No. I don't! Here, take your bag and get out.' She threw it at him.

Catching his handgrip, William yelled back. 'Why did you come then? What do you want of me?' He shook his head and left the room muttering. 'Women, I'll never understand them.'

They left the camp early the next morning and drove in silence until Marion pointed ahead. 'What's that?'

William stopped the vehicle and narrowed his eyes against the glare of the sun. He lifted the field-glasses and adjusted the focus. 'It's a leopard, it might come this way.' Lowering the binoculars he switched the engine off.

'Sit very still. I think it's a female. There might be something behind her for she seems apprehensive. It's rare for leopards to stalk on an open road. Here take a look.'

'She swings her head from side to side,' said Marion looking through the glasses.

'Most likely there is a pack of wild dogs or poachers after her. She hasn't seen us yet.'

The leopard advanced cautiously, raising puffs of fine dust beneath her paws and surveying her surroundings.

'What a contrast between the black and white markings,' whispered Marion. 'See the strength and vitality in the tendons and muscles.'

The leopard stopped in mid-stride, alerted to the sound of activity and a strange odour. Immediately, as she saw the vehicle facing her, she opened her jaws exposing curved fangs. With a harsh bark she bounded into the grass.

'Her fur is like silk reflecting in the sun. The lion may be the king of the jungle but the leopard is certainly the queen. She walks with the pride of an ancient Egyptian goddess.'

At ease behind the wheel, William nodded slowly. His thoughts far away, his eyes focused on the dusty road. 'The lion and the unicorn, I remember Hattie . . .'

'Please William not Hattie again,' Marion said clenching her fist.

'I'm sorry . . . I don't meant to . . . But I have an idea. Hattie once told me that as a child she saw a roan antelope

175

against the skyline. She saw it from the window of a train. The animal stood on a hillock, its head back and the antlers aligned as though it had only one. Its hide shone in the sunlight. She thought it was a unicorn.'

Through the trees sun-birds flitted, their feathers tinted with greens and golds. In the distance the crickets added their songs to the sounds of Africa.

'Come,' William said at last. 'I have the subject for a painting. I've found a quarry, and now need to find the predator.'

Elated, Marion smiled inwardly. The first part of her scheme might work. If William's painting is a masterpiece, she could sell the other pictures for a fortune. Now she must plan a public presentation, with William handing Isaac the painting.

Heat waves shimmered over the scrubland as they drove out of the park and onto the highway and headed north for home.

In the distance a horde of people, divided into two groups, were making their way to the historic site. The first group chanted and waved beer mugs. From one foot to the other, they hopped in a drunken dance. Women carried large plastic containers of beer on their heads which they sold along the way. Business was good, for screaming and dancing for independence was hot and thirsty work. Babies strapped to their backs slept or fretted and toddlers ran to keep up with their parents. The second group of people walked and talked earnestly among themselves. William's hands tightened on the wheel.

'Pull over to the side of the road. We'll stay here until they have passed,' Marion ordered William.

He gaped at her. 'We dare not. That rabble is looking for blood and it's not going to be mine.'

He gunned the vehicle into low gear and it shot forward. 'I hope to God, they haven't seen us.'

Chapter 19

'We must hide from this crowd, as I've nothing to defend ourselves with.' William's frown deepened as his anxiety grew. 'The gravel pit, it's our only chance! We must get there.' His voice rose as he tramped on the accelerator. Black fumes belched from the exhaust and left a trail of fetid smoke. The Jaguar, shuddering like a wounded beast, leaped forward.

'For heaven's sake William, stop panicking. You are in a sweat for nothing. Your hands are so wet you can't grip the steering wheel.'

William wiped his forehead on his sleeve and his palms on his shirt. Down the road they rushed towards the approaching mob.

'I'm not exaggerating, that mob is dangerous. We must get to that turn-off before they see us. Watch out for a track on your side of the car.'

'There it is,' Marion pointed.

Straining his arms William spun the steering wheel hard down and swung onto the rough track.

He yelled. 'Hold on. The road will get worse.'

Marion's hat slipped sideways as she grabbed onto the dashboard to save herself from crashing into the windscreen. 'William, slow . . .' screamed Marion.

Ignoring her protests, he interrupted to repeat his anxiety. 'The gravel pit is close by. Our only chance is to hide in there. Believe me, we're in trouble if that mob gets to us.'

'You are panicking for nothing. Just like you to get into a

177

flap for no reason. Why don't you turn around and go back to the park?'

'We haven't enough petrol, that's why I wanted to use the jeep. We dare not go the other way, south. Most likely there's a political rally taking place in the football stadium, it is about three miles from here, that's where this crowd is heading. We're between the two mobs.'

William cursed under his breath as stones and pebbles spattered under the low-slung chassis. The Jag fish-tailed as William hit the brakes and forced the wheels around through a narrow cutting into a deep pit. A mound of rocks brought the car to a halt.

'Get out, hurry, we might make it to the other side and climb to safety. They haven't seen us.'

Marion climbed slowly from the passenger seat and opened the rear door. She shook her head as if to say, 'Really William, you're hysterical.'

The chanting of the crowd became louder.

'Leave everything, we haven't the time. Don't you realise the danger?' William barked and pulled Marion away from the car.

'My camera, I'm not going to leave it.'

'Forget your camera, I'll buy you a dozen.'

'But those shots I took for the painting . . .'

'Come on for Christ's sake, we're in danger. Listen, they are almost above us.'

He grabbed her arm and dragged her after him. Over the rocks and sharp stones he forced her to run. Marion staggered and stumbled and tried to free herself from his grasp.

'William, I'm losing my hat!'

Disregarding her distresses, he continued to pull her over the rough terrain to a mound of rubble. He slid to a stop.

'Duck down. No, get right down.' He pushed her shoulder hard. 'We must hide here, as we will never make it to the top. Maybe they won't see us or the car.'

Crouching behind the rubble, William checked the slope of the pit behind them.

178

'If the mob sees us, we must dash up there. It's about twenty feet high; that'll be our only chance.'

Puffing and panting, Marion finally caught her breath. She rubbed at the scratches of her leg. 'William, hiding here is ridiculous. Isaac is the leader of the party and he won't let any harm come to me.'

William stared at her. Fine lines and wrinkles had deepened around his eyes. She had applied heavier makeup to hide the blemishes caused by the tropical sun.

'Isaac won't let any harm come to you!' he mimicked her. 'How do you know? What dealings have you had with him?'

'Only through business,' Marion lied. 'You saw the exquisite African art that I market. He collects pieces for me to sell and has never been familiar or discourteous. In fact he is very grateful for what I do.'

'I'm sure he is,' William replied cynically. 'He's crafty and will tell you what you want to hear.'

'Why would those people up there want to harm us?'

William sighed as he rested his back against the rubble. 'They are hungry for action and at the moment under the influence of liquor. For years now the Africans have wanted independence. Unfortunately there are some self-appointed leaders who are out for their own ends. Isaac, who is certainly very clever, is one of them. He's ambitious for power and will use his intelligence to get what he wants. Toss told me how these self-proclaimed leaders organised the rallies. They are fast talkers and skilled at persuading the people. As in most mobs, there are the hotheads and they usually demand immediate action. They smash anything in their paths. Listen, the crowd has reached the granite rock. Remember the one I told you about.'

'The sacred rock, where only a chief may stand?'

'Yes, that's right.'

'That means Isaac is a bona fide leader.'

William shrugged. 'Who knows? I know I don't like that man. He's a fraud. Toss told me.'

'How can you accept what Toss says?'

179

'Because he is close to the people and he understands their way of thinking.'

'I'm sure Isaac knows the people better than Toss. Why do you mistrust Isaac? You haven't given him a chance. He respects you.'

'I don't believe that.'

'You're a racist the way you order your servants about.'

'I'm a realist. There are men like Jourbor who I trust with my life. Hush, listen to the cheers.'

Isaac had led the first group of dancing followers to the stand of trees. There he halted the march. As he stepped onto the granite rock, the crowd yelled. Tall and dignified, Isaac made an imposing figure. A black and white striped gown covered his dark suit. His wide sleeves were draped gracefully over his arms. A round hat, decorated with chevrons of black and white added to his height.

'I will lead you in our fight for independence,' Isaac began and threw out his arms to embrace the scene. 'This is our land.'

The crowd cheered, their throats ululating and chests heaving. They waved their hands above their heads. The second group who had stayed well back arrived. They sat apart and quietly watched.

'We'll govern ourselves,' Isaac shouted above the racket. Louder came the uproar from the masses.

The orator, stretching his hand in supplication, calmed the crowd. He began his tirade.

'White settlers have raped our country,' he began. His words, clear and forceful, carried across the open fields. 'They have mined all the wealth that lay in the ground. They have stolen our gold and minerals. Now they farm the fertile lands. What have they left us with? Nothing!'

Loud and long clapping followed his speech. Isaac remained still until the crowd settled back into silence. Then he made his point. 'Our clever carvers produce wonderful art. What happens to all their work? I will tell you. The art dealers sell them and keep all the profits. The carver gets very little for his work.'

180

Heads and fists shook at this injustice.

'When we are in power, we will live in big houses, drive cars and wear smart and pretty clothes,' promised Isaac. 'We will build big schools and hospitals and hotels. Listen carefully and I tell you what we must do.'

Speaking with patience and deliberation, he explained the meaning of democracy and how to vote.

'Remember to put the mark next to the panga.' An attendant held up a large illustration of a broad cutlass. 'This is my symbol. You will be a traitor if you don't put a mark by the panga.'

From the group that sat apart there came a murmur like a gentle breeze slowly disturbing the air. Reverently a name was spoken, quietly at first then growing louder. 'M'kama. M'kama, M'kama.' Slow clapping accompanied each syllable in the name.

M'kama the hunter, the wanderer, appeared as if ascending from the mist of voices. He walked forward shaking his spear and stopped in front of Isaac.

'Who said you were a true chief?' he challenged Isaac. 'You are my son of my second wife and not a chief. What right have you to speak here on the sacred land? How dare you stand on the sacred rock?'

'M'kama . . . M'kama . . . M'kama . . .' the chanting continued. Isaac bent to his assistant holding the picture of the cutlass.

'The people respect and venerate my father. His influence can sway them. The sooner I get him back to the village the better.'

'Can you persuade him to go?'

'I'll think of something. Bribe him with a fresh leopard pelt. That is his badge of office.'

M'kama called to Isaac. 'What is this democracy, this freedom of which you speak? Where is the freedom if we *must* vote for you?'

The crowd became restless. Perspiration poured down Isaac's cheeks as he glanced about. He had to find an answer to save face. How could he pacify the crowd?

181

M'kama banished his spear and asked one more question. 'If the white farmers leave who will grown enough corn and produce meat for all the people?'

Not knowing how to reply, Isaac faltered and the mob swayed restlessly.

'You are too old to ask such questions,' he shouted back, 'we must stop such talk. Kill it . . .'

A cry rang out, saving Isaac embarrassing explanations. The horde rose as one and surged forward to the edge of the gravel pit.

A youth pointed to William's Jag. 'Look there.'

With Isaac's last word 'kill' ringing in their ears, the mob went hysterical. Down the road they rushed. Pulsating like a giant spider with hundreds of pairs of brown legs and arms. Its body spotted in red, green and white clothing. It oozed through the narrow gap and spread out again into a bulbous mass, sliding to the car.

William and Marion peeped over the mound of rubble. They watched a woman unstrap her infant from her back. She placed the infant on the ground and went to the back of the Jag. Grappling with the handle of the boot she finally opened it. A man tried to snatch the bags but she pushed him aside. Grabbing the luggage, she dashed through the crowd. Her infant sat happily banging the hub-cap with a stone. Above the child, two youths fought over the camera and field-glasses.

Out of the crowd came a man wearing a grease-stained coverall. He wrenched the petrol cap off the Jag and dipped a cloth into the fuel. Onto the back seat he tossed the petrol-soaked rag. Then he dropped a lighted match on to the cloth and immediately pressed his way back into the crowd. Flames and smoke began to bellow from the car. The crowd pushed and shoved those behind to get a away from the heat.

William gaped with horror. 'These people, they love fires. Oh God there's a kid by the wheel.' He got up and ordered Marion. 'Stay here, don't move.'

Slipping and sliding on the gravel, he ran and snatched the

182

child from certain death. Behind a small pile of rocks, he threw himself down, and protected the child with his body. The windows cracked as the oxygen became depleted inside the car. An explosion echoed round the pit. Fifteen minutes of belching smoke passed before the mob rose slowly and edged up to William. Holding the baby, he stood his ground and tried to read their faces. His end would be quick if he showed the slightest sign of fear.

Death on the battlefield was familiar to him. Horrific sounds and smells of heated metal made him recall the war. Visions of bombing and artillery fire erupting about him. Dead and maimed men were still a vivid memory. He had once faced a hostile army far superior to this raggle-taggle horde before him. Yet a raging crowd waving their raised pangas, axes and clubs was more threatening. The crowd swayed. From the corner of his eye William saw a movement, a man closing in. He swung round and stared the aggressor down.

A smell of unwashed bodies and sweat mingled in the arid air. The stench wafted over the pit. The enemy smelled blood. William had no weapons to protect himself, only courage and very little time. He scanned the faces in front of him. He must recognise one.

'Gladys,' he commanded. 'What are you doing here?'

Embarrassed by the recognition, Gladys covered her face. The crowd stepped back.

William faced her. 'You should be at home. Take this child and give it back to its mother, then you get home.'

William advanced fearlessly into the crowd and handed the child to Gladys and walked away with measured steps.

At Marion's side, he spoke in a precise voice. 'Don't look back. Walk steadily up the bank.'

Marion faltered, about to object.

'Keep moving,' he commanded.

'Listen,' she said, 'there's another truck coming.'

'That might be more supporters arriving. We are in real trouble now.'

183

A woman's voice sounded above the confusion. 'That's the beer truck!'

The crowd turned and pushed back through the cutting.

William and Marion reached the top of the slope. They looked back at the shell of the Jag.

'I promised to drive Emma to her wedding in the Jag.' William said and sadly shook his head. 'Oh God! How much more must I lose?'

With shoulders drooping, William walked ahead through the low scrub until they came to a back road.

Marion caught up with him. 'I hear a vehicle – listen.'

'You're right, now where do we hide?'

The sound grew louder. Nearer and nearer it came, until a blue van pulled up beside them.

The driver struck his head out the window. A ray of sunlight made a halo of his frizzy ginger hair. His eyes blinked and the nose wiggled. Frowns came and went. His lips twitched twice before he said.

'Trouble Baas?'

William spoke through the window of the van. 'Yes, back there.' He pointed over his shoulder with his thumb. 'The natives are not too friendly, as the old saying goes.'

'Ya, man. I heard from by boss-boy. Said there waz t' be a drunk-up at the stadium. Bloody political nonsense. There are these rallies all over the place. Nothing much comes of them, just bloody drunk-ups. Wanta ride, your missus looks done in.' He stretched over and opened the door.

'Yes, thanks. They burned my car in the gravel pit.' William helped Marion into the van and squeezed beside her. Speaking over her head, he said, 'I'm Auston-Jones. I live on the other side of Ashvale. Where are you off to?'

'Me, I'm Pete. I'm taking these back roads 'cos I wannta get to The Junction tonight. Maybe it's too dangerous with all these drunks on the road.'

'Can you get us into town, to Mr Anderson's place? It's this side of the city, on Third Avenue.'

'Ya, sure no problem, man. I know where Third is.' Pete checked the rear mirror and pulled on to the road.

184

'Where do you work?' asked William.

'I'm my own boss, carting and contracting. As a kid I lived in Joburg . . .'

'That's Johannesburg,' William translated for Marion.

'. . . during the depression I carted luggage for a fat lady to the station. I remember she had two kids with her. One with big funny coloured eyes. The other was skinny and had knobbly knees. It's funny what you remember as a kid.' Pete's face twitched again before he continued. 'I got fourpence, four shiny pennies for carrying the trunk. I guess carrying goods got into my blood then. When the war started, I joined up with the Coloured Corps. Spent it up North. With the cash me and my boetie . . .'

'That's friend or brother,' William interrupted again for Marion's sake.

'Doesn't she speak English?' Pete pointed a nicotine-stained finger at Marion.

William smiled. 'Yes, but a different kind of English.'

'Funny kinna English.' Pete shrugged. 'Me and my boetie haul goods from here to The Junction and farther down the road.'

Pete chatted as he drove William and Marion to the Anderson's house.

'Will you hang on for a moment and drive me home?' William said.

'That's no problem, I'll stay in the city for the night. It'll be safer to go on in the morning.'

'You can stay at my house. I'd like to pay you for the petrol.'

'Agh nie, it's okay Baas. I'll go to my boetie's place.'

William spoke to Marion. 'Hang on here, I'll see if Andy is in.'

Pete stared blatantly at Marion's hips.

'Have ya any kids?' he asked.

Marion blushed in anger and turned away and saw William walking up the path.

At the door he pressed the bell and waited, tapping his

185

thumb against his teeth anxiously. Eventually Andy Anderson came to the door.

'My boy, you look awful! What happened to you?' he said smoothing down his ruffled hair. William explained quickly and Andy nodded.

Back at the van William helped Marion out. 'Do you want to come in for a drink?' he asked Pete.

'No thanks Baas, I'll wait here.'

Andy stood aside at the door. He said to Marion, 'Come in. Come in.'

'Andy, let Marion fill you in,' William instructed them. 'Then phone the police. Tell them to go to my place, they will get there before me. I'm worried about Gladys, she may get home before me. God knows who she may bring with her and what they might do.'

'Yes, of course,' Andy answered.

'Marion, stay here tonight,' he ordered her. 'I'm sure Mrs Anderson will fix you up with some nightclothes.'

Marion glared at William. 'No, I will go with you. Really William, I don't know how you got me into this. Dragging me across the gravel pit and leaving me with that . . . that individual in the car.'

William frowned at her.

'We'll sort that out later,' he spoke harshly. 'Listen to me, it's too dangerous. I want you to stay here until the rally is over. You can't stay alone, not after what happened. I'm sure the Andersons will have you. Does Isaac know where you live?'

Marion's eyes flashed but William ignored her and, without waiting for an answer, said, 'Will that be okay with you, Andy?'

'Yes, of course, we'll do all we can.'

'I'll get going then. I'm anxious about the children.' William walked a few steps. He turned, went back and stood in front of Marion. Touching her cheek, he said, 'I'm sorry about last night and what happened today. I was insensitive. I'll make it up to you. Come out to my place next week.'

He turned around and went back to the van.

186

'Take care of the paintings,' she called out.

William halted at the van with his hand on the catch.

'My God, is that her only concern? Now I see a finished picture: I've the subjects, the hunted and the hunter. I'm the prey.' He wrenched open the car door.

Chapter 20

Marion found William asleep on the couch. His hand hung over the edge and his fingers touching the floor. She noticed for the first time the greying of his hair about the temples and the fatigue that yellowed the taut skin across his cheekbones. He lay with his unshaven chin pressed to his shoulder, his breathing was shallow as it came in short gasps through bloodless lips.

Once again, it was at his invitation that she came to the house. She had rung the bell at the front door and waited until Jourbor answered her ring. Surly and without greeting her, he pointed to the lounge. The room felt empty at first then she heard shallow and irregular breathing. Tiptoeing farther into the room, she looked over the back of the couch and saw William asleep. Where was his painting? It was not in the lounge. What had he been up to? There was no evidence of drink. An artist's paraphernalia littered a table by the window. Paint had spilled onto the floor and carried across the carpet by his footprints. He had accomplished nothing.

'Damn him. What will it take to get him motivated? There is very little time left.' Marion's temper flared as she flounced out of the lounge into the dining-room, where Jourbor had re-hung *Old Mr Auston-Jones*. A shudder ran down her back as she turned to go but something was amiss. The chairs were out of place. The silver vase on the table obscured something. She went forward, around the furniture. William's canvas leaned against the back of a chair.

189

'My God! He's done it.' Marion held her hands to her face and repeated her words. 'He's done it. He has created a marvel.'

Sensing a movement behind her, she glanced quickly over her shoulder. William stood there, slouching against the door frame with his hands in his pockets and his eyebrows raised in question.

'Well, what do you think?' he asked quietly.

'Magnificent. It's . . . sensational.'

Marion pressed her hand against her lips trying to assimilate her words. How could she describe such beauty?

'How unlike your previous work. The composition, texture, colour, and style is so different and that makes it remarkable. You've created reality on the canvas. This is a masterpiece. It will be an ideal token of goodwill. The ambassador – HE – will be grateful for such a gift.'

'Take it and give it to him.'

'You do know the reason he wants it?'

William repeated harshly. 'Yes. Take it and give it to him.' He turned to leave the room.

Marion called after him. 'No. I can't give it to him. HE must present it to Isaac. After all, Isaac is the leader of the party. I'm sure Rona told to you about the presentation.'

William returned to the room, frowning. 'She said something about auctioning it for charity, the wildlife organisation.'

'I'm sorry William. Didn't she make herself clear? You know Rona, how she gets muddled at times. HE wishes to present it at a reception. He wants all the prominent citizens and the news media to be there.'

Marion walked to the far end of the room, embarrassed to face him when she lied. 'The invitations are printed.'

With head thrust forward and eyes blazing in anger, William repeated. 'Invitations printed! Where will this function take place?'

Marion ran her tongue over her red lips and gave a little smile. A vision of Isaac accepting William's masterpiece, here in William's house, blinded her for a moment. She went up close. She wanted to see the anger in William's face.

'Here,' she gloated, savouring the moment.

William clenched his fist and turned from her.

'No! Why can't you leave us be?'

'Please,' altering her attitude like a chameleon changing its colour.

She implored graciously. 'Please, do it for your friends. They deserve a kind gesture. Haven't they stood by you, mourned with you? You must thank them for all their kindness. Do it, Hattie would like that. And you owe me, you said so yourself.'

'What do I owe Hattie, my friends or you? Go, take it. It is yours.'

Covering his face with his hands, he lamented, 'How much more must I give of myself? Oh God, why? Nothing's the same.'

Marion went to him, took his hands in hers and spoke quietly.

'It cannot be. For the sake of your children, work through your grief.' She lifted her beautiful face, the green eyes beseeching. 'They can't live in a house full of memories. This place is so still, it's like a morgue. They don't deserve this.'

Mesmerized by her liquid green eyes, fluorescent like the waves, William whispered. 'Eyes, it's the eyes that get you.'

'Forget the past.' Marion's voice was low, compelling and cunning.

'How can I? It's always with me.' William walked away from her. 'My past comes into my dreams. Dreams of the sea and officers talking about eyes. Eyes that haunt me. Go and do what you want!' William walked from the room.

'I need money for the reception,' Marion called after him and rubbed the palm of her hands together.

'Dreams . . . I dream. Tell Andy, he's my accountant. He will give you your money.'

William went back to his sofa and buried his face in his arms.

191

'Rona, I need your advice,' said Marion charged with energy and excitement. At last she had control of William's money and his household. 'The house and garden must be completely different. Last time the guests were here it was for Hattie's funeral. I certainly don't want any reminders of that.'

This was the first of many discussions Marion would have with Rona. The elder lady shared Marion's excitement and agreed with the project. She lifted her cup and took a sip of her tea.

'You're right. Be a dear, tell me when is the reception?'

'Two weeks from today and there's so much to be done.'

'What alterations will you make?' Rona pulled at her cardigan and gave Marion her full attention.

'I'll have the wall between the two lounges removed. That will make a room big enough for the reception. I have ordered suitable carpeting to cover the complete floor. I loathed that parquet flooring in the dining-room. I'll replace the floor as well.'

'And the fixtures, are you changing those?'

'Oh yes, definitely, and I have selected furnishings to complement the new carpets. William's painting will be on the dais at the back of the room. The guests will stand to the side and the buffet set opposite.' Marion made a mental note not to forget red velvet material to drape over the picture.

'My! You have done wonders. Now tell me about your menu.'

'I am not serving the usual fare. I've ordered smoked salmon from the cute . . .' Once that was their personal joke, her and William's, 'the cute little shop.' Marion shuddered.

'Something the matter, dear?' asked Rona.

'No. Only there's someone stamping on my grave.'

With Marion directing operations, the rebuilding of William's house began. Bricklayers, carpenters, painters and plasterers hurried in and out from dawn late into the night.

Early into the second week, Marion heard Jack shouting.

'Liam,' he called. 'Liam come see, there's a big lorry in the garden. It has crashed into the hedge and landed in the frog pond.'

192

The boys rushed out the house and tripped up a worker. The roll of carpeting went spinning into the dust.

Marion had paused in her frenzy of activities to plead sweetly with William.

'The children are hindering the workers, especially Jack. He is becoming too excited. I'm afraid they might get hurt.'

She followed up her reasoning in a voice loaded with accusations. 'We don't want Liam on his pony to cause another accident, do we?'

Liam ducked in time to avoid the long red fingernails stretched out to ruffle his hair.

'Why are you changing the house, Daddy?' complained Jack as they walked away. 'It's horrible.'

'I don't know how I got into this mess,' William confessed softly. 'It will soon be over.'

He stopped, gazing into the distance, seeing into the future and spoke with confidence, his voice strong:

'When the party is over, I will rebuild the house completely. Enlarge the stables, buy more horses. Use the land for a research station, to increase the yields of corn. The population needs food, not paintings. For too long I have only considered my pleasures. It's the future that is important now. I've work to do. So much to be done and we have so little time.'

'Daddy, Daddy,' Emma pulled at her father's jacket. 'You promised to take us to the seaside.'

'Yes, I did, my sweetheart.' William caressed the little face. 'I'll take you to the sea. There you can play on the sand and make mud pies. Come, I remember a stream on the other side of the fields. Let's see if we can find it.'

William rediscovered places where he spent his childhood. The tree with a hollow trunk where he hid from his father's torments and ridicule. He found the stream and the weeping mutepe tree. Clear water flowed gently over white pebbles.

'May we bring our nets and fish here tomorrow?' asked Liam. William nodded. The following day Liam caught a small silver fish.

'It's so pretty,' he said as he released it back into the water.

193

William and the children climbed to the top of Pioneer Hill. Liam surveyed the view and pointed to the city. 'I can see Mr Anderson's office building. It's the highest building.'

'Which one? Show me,' cried Emma.

Liam lifted his little sister. 'There. Can you see the stream where we fished?'

'There's Jourbor sitting by the boiler and there is the jacaranda tree,' said Jack. 'Look at all the trucks in the front of the house. What are they bringing to the house?'

'More carpets and furniture,' answered William with a sigh. When would this upheaval of their lives end, William wondered. Oh, he wished to be free of Marion and all her intrigues.

'Over there,' Liam pointed, 'on that low hill is the cem . . .' Liam stopped. He and Jack looked at their father. William nodded sadly.

'Tell me, Liam, what's on the hill?' Emma hopped up and down.

'Never mind. Come let's play.' Jack took her hand. 'You can hide first, I'll count.'

William sat on a granite rock while Jack and Emma played their games. The games had rules too complicated for an adult's mind. William methodically retied Liam's shoelaces. Patiently, with folded arms he sat, waiting to repeat the process. Liam found a spent cartridge and showed it to his father.

'It's a small one. What sort of gun did it come from?'

Weighing the cartridge in his hand, William jiggled it up and down. 'From an old type of hand gun, probably owned by a pioneer. I wonder who used it up here?'

Taking the spent cartridge, Liam studied it, turning it over and over before pitching it over the rocks. Emma came up and repeated her childish questions. William tickled her gently and answered them with equanimity.

'It's time we went.' William called to the children. 'I'll carry Jack. Liam can you piggy-back Emma?'

As they made their way down the hill, William quietly sang the songs he learned as a choirboy. His songs were about the sea and far-away places and ancient times. With his head against his father's shoulder Jack listened. Though not understanding the words, the voice calmed him, as once his mother's did – so many years ago.

They passed the paddock and stepped over the broken fence. At the hitching post William checked the locks on the boys' cycles. Jourbor always waited for them at the kitchen door. Laughing and calling, the children ran to him. Pioneer Hill became the children's favourite playground. The warm and fresh air, unpolluted by builders' dust and harsh voices, lifted their spirits.

On the day of the party they started down the hill as usual. William picking his way over the rough path, glanced up. He stopped singing.

'Liam, we must go the other way. We'll go down the other path,' he said.

'Why Dad? It's farther and Emma is getting heavy.'

'Listen to me,' William spoke harshly.

Liam grumbled, 'Okay.'

Jack said. 'Put me down, I'll walk, I'm better now.'

William lifted Emma up and hurried forward. The boys slipped and scrambled over the stones to keep up with him on the unfamiliar path.

'Go to Jourbor,' said William when he set Emma down. 'I'll be along soon.'

He went into the house and found Marion, suitably dressed in slacks and matching blouse, in the passage. Signing a document with a flourish, she passed it to a delivery man.

'You won't let me down, be here by six. Off you go then.' She faced William. 'Oh there you are. You're late. Your new dress suit is in your room. I don't want you to wear that old one.'

'You meddling bitch,' William yelled.

Unruffled, Marion sneered at him. Poised and relaxed she removed an imaginary speck of dust from her blouse and disregarded his verbal abuse.

'By the way, I have bought the imported smoked salmon for the banquet. It will be the centrepiece. Okay?'

195

'The jacaranda! Why? Marion, why did you destroy it?' he shouted. The pangs of agony twisted deep in his gut.

'Oh, for Heaven's sake, calm down, William. It was old and dangerous. It could fall and hurt the children.' Marion tossed her dark hair from her shoulders.

'Why didn't you tell me?' he shouted hysterically.

Marion's eyes flashed. 'Don't scream at me. Where are you these days? You do nothing to help. I take all the responsibility. Stop your screaming, it's late, Toss is already here.'

'You bitch . . . I'll . . .' William shrieked. His eyes blazed red.

Toss rushed to his side. 'Hold on, old man. Come I'll help you to change and I have a drink poured for you.'

'Now children,' Marion said, 'into bed and I want you to be quiet as little mice. Your father's friends are coming this evening. And we don't want to spoil his party, do we?'

The three children sat on their beds and gazed at her with blank expressions.

'Mama let us go to the party,' said Emma. 'Daddy will let us come if I ask him.'

'No. Not this time.' Marion's frown frightened the little girl.

'I want my . . .' Emma began to cry.

'There, there don't cry.' Marion quickly changed her expression and gave the child a sweet smile. 'Next time you can come to the party, I promise you. Tomorrow you can make mud pies. Go to sleep now. Liam, come here.'

The boy climbed from his bed and went with Marion to the door.

'Here are five pounds. If you keep the children quiet, I'll give you another five.'

Liam shrugged. 'Okay, I'll try.'

'Good, off to bed with you. I must be with your father to welcome the guests.'

William and Marion received the guests at the front door. Her evening gown fell gracefully to the floor.

William looked calm and composed. An hour ago Toss

had said. 'You're knackered old man. Here drink this.' He handed William a glass of dark liquid.

William swallowed the mixture in one gulp. 'What the hell was that?'

'Something to ease the pain. You'll look and feel better in a moment.'

The potion served its purpose for William had calmed down. He stood up straight and smiled a welcome to the guests.

Marion tapped her foot irritably.

'Jourbor should be out there directing the cars. I bought him a doorman's uniform. Now he is nowhere to be seen.'

William shrugged and held out his hand to the approaching guests.

'How pretty with all the coloured lights around the pillars. The house is so different,' said Betsy Montecland in admiration. 'Marion, you are so good for William. How well he looks.'

'Splendid, splendid,' said Charlie. He shook hands with all those around him then bounced up the steps.

His Excellency arrived. He held Marion's hand. 'William is his old self. You have worked wonders, my dear.'

'Thank you. Isaac will be here shortly.'

Isaac arrived later. His retinue, all dressed in long colourful robes, trooped behind him.

'I can only stay a moment,' he said as he held Marion's outstretched hand. 'I must take my elderly father back to his village early tomorrow.' Isaac leaned over Marion and kissed her cheek. She blushed and looked around quickly. Who had seen?

The guests filed into the lounge. They were aware of the soft luxurious carpet under their feet and the richly decorated room. Champagne sparkled in crystal glasses and delicacies were arranged on silver platters. Andy Anderson and his wife stood to one side.

'What has that bitch done?' exclaimed Andy, 'this place looks like a bloody circus.'

'Hush,' answered his wife. 'It's none of our business.'

197

'I shouldn't have listened to William. Do you know she has spent a great deal of his money and somehow she will get the rest of it. How astutely she has used us all. Played on our friendship, on Rona's misdirected goodwill, and his standing in the community. What did William do to her I wonder? She used the children and Hattie's memory to manipulate him. Why, can you tell me, why? What is she after?'

Chapter 21

'Hush Andy, not so loud,' answered Mrs Anderson soothingly. 'We'll never know how this all came about. I'm sure Isaac's involved somehow. Look at him, decked out in that long robe, with the hem flapping at his heels. Is that robe traditional wear?'

'Look at William. I've never known him to be so aware of his strength. Last week he said, "I must work for our future. It's up to me to lead the way." I wonder what he means?'

'Such troubling times,' sighed Mrs Anderson as she glanced around, 'but you are right, the place is like a bloody circus.'

Voices rose and compliments flowed around the elderly couple.

'How lovely, just like a showroom.'

'. . . and the buffet. My oh my. See the spun sugar decorating the eclairs.'

'The salads and desserts. What perfection!'

'Remember the last time we were here, at Hattie's wake. What a difference.'

'Splendid, splendid.'

'Where's William's painting? I can't wait to see it.'

'It's on the dais.'

Conversations flowed, guests sipped their drinks and nibbled at the snacks.

Crystal and silverware glittered on the damask tablecloth. Every platter and dish held mouth-watering offerings, each offering impeccably co-ordinated with the centrepiece.

199

Thirty inches of smoked salmon lay on a bed of crushed ice, glorified in death. A splinter of light gave life to its eyes.

Through the ohs and ahs came children's shrilling and laughter.

'I'll go to them, darling,' said Marion sarcastically and touched William's arm. 'You entertain the guests.'

Marion beamed and nodded graciously as she glided through the guests and up the stairs. She flung open the bedroom door to see the room in a shambles. Toys, books and clothing littered the floor. Jack was at the peak of his upward bounce as he jumped on his bed. Down he came, to land on his stomach and scramble to the far end of the bed. He grabbed Our Haggerty and gaped at Marion. Emma crawled under the covers as fast as she could.

Hands on hips Marion raised herself to her full height. Liam was horrified at her contorted features as she shook her long finger at him. His picture books never illustrated a furious Egyptian queen. The frowns and narrowed eyes made her really ugly. He shuddered at the hideous painted claws and distorted face.

'You promised me Liam, to keep these two quiet,' she hissed. 'And you,' she singled out Jack, 'are a disobedient little brat.' She snatched Our Haggerty out of his arms. 'You've disobeyed me. Now you'll never see this again.'

The door banged behind her. The children heard the bathroom door open and shut. They sat very still, petrified.

Smoothing her hair to calm herself, Marion went back to the reception.

'Do have another snack, David,' she purred before mingling with the crowd.

'I don't mind if I do,' David Bentwood popped a morsel into his mouth, his grey beard wiggling as he chewed.

A tinkling sound hushed the chatter and the guests arranged themselves in a semi-circle facing His Excellency and Isaac on the dais, the draped painting between them.

'Friends,' the ambassador's voice held a smile. 'First we must thank Marion and William for this wonderful reception.'

'Hear. Hear,' the guests chanted in unison.

'And we know who did all the work,' he went on. All raised their glasses to Marion. She bestowed a gracious nod to acknowledge her due.

'It's my honour to present this gift to Isaac, the leader of the new political party.' The ambassador pulled the golden tasselled cord and the red velvet curtain fell away to reveal the painting.

Obscure contours of jackals and hyaenas showed through distant heat-waves. Foreshortened in the centre was a roan antelope in the prime of its life. Its regal head was thrown back and the strong and majestic antlers curved over its body. Russet sheen on the hide was accented in the hazy sunlight. Smoky brown eyes stared in supplication. Pleading for a chance for liberty from the savage predator.

Not a word nor a gesture came from the guests. They remained still and astounded as if bearing witness to a miracle until voices broke the spell.

'The leopard, the predator, is it leaping from the picture?'

'Those drops of blood on the claws are red as rubies.'

'Its cruel green eyes sparkle with greed.'

Subdued comments on the painting continued:

'See the white and black markings, they give me a feeling of movement.'

'The muscles ripple.'

'Hush HE is speaking.'

'With great . . .' He got no further.

A scream came from the floor. Jack stood in the centre of the gathering. One hand held up his pyjama pants while the other pointed at Marion. His russet curls formed a halo about his head.

'You,' he screamed, his face contorted in anger. 'You stole Our Haggerty. You wanted Our Haggerty!'

Mouths dropped open. Wavelengths of shock rippled through the air. Eyes widened with astonishment at the small accuser. Did he say Hattie or Haggerty? Had God, in his wrath, sent this cherub to denounce the Jezebel? Four chubby fingers, each representing Hattie's protectors, were pointed

201

at Marion. One finger for Emma, the little chaperone. Another for Liam the dashing knight on his pony. The third for Jourbor's strength through the voice of the drums. And, lastly, one finger representing Jack, the denouncer.

'You stole Our Haggerty,' the hysterical child screamed again. 'Give me back my Haggerty.'

William pushed his way through the company and gathered his son in his arms.

'Come Jack, we'll find Our Haggerty,' he comforted the boy as he walked from the room.

Crack! A crystal goblet, a family heirloom, snapped at the stem. All heads turned to see the base of the wine glass fall at Marion's feet. She disregarded the remains of the broken glass in her hand and looked around for sympathy. Isaac was there, surely he would come forward to alleviate the humiliation. She was wrong. He made no move to help her. Raising his head a fraction, he looked down his nose at her. The thin lips curled into a sardonic smile. The only emotion she saw in his hooded eyes was ridicule. Marion stormed to the door. On her way out she paused for a second and threw the broken goblet into the salmon. It landed with a quiet plop.

Down the steps she ran, her beautiful gown dragging over the gravel. At her car she yanked the door open.

'All for nothing. All for bloody nothing. Damn you Hattie. Damn you. Oh God! To be on that plane, out of this bloody country. Tomorrow I'll start packing and by next week I'll be back in a civilised country.'

Marion sat in her car weeping hot tears of anger and degradation. A light went on in an upstairs room. William, with his little boy pressed to his shoulder, was silhouetted against the light. Marion glared at the figures, hate surging through her. Loathing for the father and his son. Stamping on the accelerator, she backed the car from the car park and drove away.

With diplomacy, the ambassador, Toss and Andy encouraged the guests to leave.

'I'll take the picture,' said Isaac.

202

'No! Come for it later, get your people out of here,' said Toss and firmly took hold of Isaac's arm and led him to the door.

'Hang in, old chap. Here's another whisky.' William took the glass from Toss.

'Someone should stay with him,' Andy said.

'No. Leave him alone. Besides Jourbor is here, he'll take care of him. Let's get the rest of this crowd home.'

William wandered through the house as if in search of someone. In the kitchen he saw Jourbor huddled in a corner. A greasy, green-coloured uniform lay at his feet. Gold braiding caught the dull light. William, in a trance, found himself in the bedroom. For a while he sat on the bed wondering why a chair was by the wardrobe door. Who had stood on it and ransacked the cupboard? All the contents lay scattered over the floor. Hattie's blue jewel box lay upside down against the leg of the bed.

William got up and left the room. He couldn't deal with the mystery, not in his present state of mind. Down the staircase and into the passage he weaved until he came to the screen door. At first it resisted opening until he gave it a sharp tug. He stepped onto the side veranda. The divan had disappeared, Gladys slept on it now in her quarters. He searched for the step, the one that needed mending. It had gone. The railings and the ivy lay crushed by builders' rubble. Gravel filled the frog pond and covered the flower-bed. Someone had pulled up the hedge to extend the car park. Only the hitching post remained, supporting the bicycles.

William went back into the house. Dazed and exhausted he rested his head against the doorjamb, and closed his eyes. Slowly, he slipped down and fell asleep on the floor.

At sunrise Gladys awoke from her drunken sleep. She climbed off the divan, staggered out of her quarters and relieved herself at the side of the building. Half squatting she dried her thighs between her legs with the front of her skirt. The wet patch left a dark stain on the cloth.

Her duty the night before was to wash the glasses and

203

send them back to the lounge. Instead, she drank all the dregs and dropped the glasses into the sink. With each drink she became more resentful. William had made a fool of her at the rally. No one ever considered her. As children, her brother, Isaac, got all the attention. Now he was a big shot and telling her what to do.

'Steal that clasp for me, Marion won't do it,' Isaac had ordered months ago. Gladys refused. He nagged her again after Hattie died. A week ago he said to her:

'At the reception, steal it then. No one will see you.'

With the party in progress she took another gulp of dregs. 'I'll look for the clasp when the kids are asleep.'

She drank some more and became too inebriated to climb the staircase. Instead she staggered out of the house and had gone to her bed.

The early morning sun warmed her. After stretching, she strolled into the kitchen and surveyed the debris from the aftermath of the party. Dirty dishes overflowed the counters. It was in the lounge she found bottle of gin. With this in hand she made her way upstairs.

In the first bedroom Marion's dress-case lay open on the bed. Between sips from the bottle, Gladys inspected each article of clothing. Holding up a bra she shook her head. 'No tits, these white bitches,' and dropped the sliver of lace onto the floor. She lit a cigarette and tossed the match after the garment.

Between swigs from the bottle she carelessly tossed lighted cigarettes over the floor. Marion's skirt caught her attention. She squeezed into it and fumbled with the zipper. Finally, she staggered down the staircase to find more liquor. The odour of the buffet came from the table. In disgust she threw a box of burning matches on the damask cloth and went back to her quarters.

William awoke and became conscious of the cramps in his limbs. He stretched his arms as the heat from fire hit him. Flames from the bedrooms meshed with the fire from the lounge. The glass on the portrait of the old man cracked, while flames licked at every painting in the narrow room.

204

Each canvas slowly curled as the oil paint melted. Part of the roof collapsed in smoke and turmoil of timber and mortar.

'The children! My god, the children!' William leaped up. Protecting his face with his arms, he rushed to the stairs. He never made it. Someone grabbed his legs and tripped him. William's chin hit the bottom step, compressing three vertebrae in the neck.

'No bwana, it's too late!' yelled Jourbor above the roar. He dragged William's inert body out of the inferno and lay it against the stump of the jacaranda tree. Then the eruption shook the remaining walls. The boiler exploded, sending fragments of metal high into the air.

Jourbor protected their faces against the sudden glare. As the glow faded, he rocked William against his chest and wailed.

'Bwana, bwana. What happened? Are the gods angry with me because I stole my river god's scarf? The lilac one, it was as soft as thistledown. My mother, she always wanted a scarf like that. A scarf to wear around her head.'

Jourbor held William's firmly against his breast. 'I'll take you to my mother's house. She will give you dark medicine. You will forget all and the pain will go. We will sit by her fire.'

Tears rolled down the noble face. Instant pictures of the past came back to Jourbor. The children at play and William painting on the veranda. He remembered Hattie's cool hand on his fevered brow as he lay sweating with malaria. All was lost. Now master and servant sat by the stump of the tree.

Gladys decided to visit her mother. She came through the smoke hobbling, for Marion's tight skirt impeded her walk. A cigarette hung from her mouth and she held a bottle in her hand. Jourbor gently laid William down and marching up to Gladys slapped her across the face.

'You black bitch!' He slapped her again and again. 'You black bitch! The children.'

She struggled out of his clasp and pointed with the bottle. 'Kangera. Kangera. Look, look.'

She waggled the bottle as he lifted his hand to slap her

again. Twisting around, he looked to where she pointed. Something was missing. He frowned. The hitching post. The bicycles had gone. He pushed her from him, ran to William and lifted him by the shoulders.

'Come, bwana, the children have gone, they are safe. We'll find them.'

William's head dropped forward – the puppet's string broken. Jourbor froze at the sight of the lifeless body. Unconscious of the smoke and heat drifting across his face, Jourbor curled into the foetus position and wept.

'Mother, I'm cold. Where is your warm fire? Mother. Mother, I want to come home.'

Chapter 22

While Jourbor grieved for his master and mistress, the children were in the marketplace. Liam, regretting his hasty decision of the night before, pushed his cycle while Jack and Emma trailed behind.

The night before William had carried Jack up the stairs and back to bed. Without looking at them he commanded. 'Go to sleep n . . . now, we will talk in the m . . . morning.' His eyes were stony and his features twisted as if in agony.

'What's wrong with Daddy? His eyes are funny and his face is all crunched up,' said Emma as William stumbled from the room.

'Hush, he's mad at Jack,' answered Liam. 'I remember he was once mad at me. His face went all twisted and his eyes turned cold and piercing. It frightened me so much I obeyed every order he gave me. We must think of something to tell him. I promised Mama to take care of you and Emma. I don't want Dad to be angry with you, Jack.'

'He's been mad since Mama left us. Is it the stuff from the funny-shaped bottle?'

'Maybe. Hush now Emma.'

'Jack looks sick.'

'Hush!' Liam repeated.

Jack sat huddled on the edge of the bed. He pouted and swung his legs and crushed Our Haggerty to his shoulder. Tears filled his eyes.

'It's not Dad that I'm afraid of, it's Marion. I'm sure she hurt Mama somehow. Marion is horrible and cruel. I hate

207

the way she walks, with all her black hair piled high she looks like a long-legged spider stalking us. I know she will always remember what I did.'

Liam shivered. 'I wonder what she will tell Dad?'

'Tell us Liam, about Uncle Seth and how he made Mama laugh,' said Emma in a small voice.

Liam began the tale once more but there was no joy in it. He came to a stop.

'I'm scared of Marion, let's go to Uncle Seth. He took care of Mama when she was little,' Jack pleaded.

'How can we get there?'

''Member Jack,' Emma said. 'Daddy wanted to tie me in a parcel and post me.'

'Mama sent Uncle Seth a parcel with Oparee, the bus driver. Uncle Seth collects his post from the store,' Jack recalled. 'Can't we catch the bus? Oparee will take care of us and we can wait at The Junction until Uncle Seth comes.'

Liam scratched his head and frowned while he considered the question. This was a way to run from Marion because he knew she would chastise them unmercifully. He had to take Emma and Jack away.

'Okay. We'll get up early tomorrow and catch the bus. Now go to sleep, I must think.'

'We'll wrap ourselves in paper like parcels,' said Emma.

Liam sighed, girls were tiresome. 'No. We can't do that.'

She began to sob. 'I wanta . . .'

'Let's pretend we're parcels,' Jack suggested.

The little girl brightened up immediately.

'Okay,' she said and twisting onto her tummy she soon went to sleep.

Jack sat thinking for a while.

'Go to sleep now, Jack,' insisted Liam.

'In a minute.'

Climbing out of bed he went to the door.

'Jack, don't cause any trouble. Come back to bed.'

Jack waved Liam quiet and crept down the passage. Ten minutes later he returned and got into bed and soon fell asleep.

In the grey light of morning Liam found the two children in the kitchen. Slipping into his tennis shoes, Liam asked, 'What are you doing?'

'Got some bread and jam to take with us. Come let's go.' Jack stuffed the newspaper package in the pocket of his new suit. He straightened his tie and commented, 'You'll be cold in your khaki shorts and thin shirt.'

Liam looked at his sister. 'You can't wear all those clothes! And those are Dad's medals. How did you get them?'

'I'm a parcel all wrapped up and these are the stamps. I found them on the bedroom floor.'

'Come on,' said Jack urgently, 'someone will wake up.'

They slipped out of the kitchen and passed the boiler. On their way to the garage, Jack suddenly stopped. 'The tree! Look what they did to the jacaranda tree!'

'The garden of dahlias, it's gone,' cried Liam in dismay. 'They are taking everything away from us.'

'Hurry, let's go. Gladys is coming out of her room,' said Jack blinded by his tears.

Liam lifted Emma on the cross bar and pushed off and Jack followed with Our Haggerty tied to the handlebars. The children cycled along the same footpath that Jourbor had taken many years ago from the market.

'Hurry up, Emma,' Liam said. 'We must cross the street to get to the bus depot.'

'I'm tired and thirsty,' she grumbled and tripped over her long skirt.

At last they arrived at the depot where passengers milled around a dilapidated bus. Workers hoisted packages and bulging suitcases onto the roof of the vehicle and secured them with coarse brown rope. Lastly, they tied a bicycle precariously to the side of the bus. The spinning wheels caught a glint of sunlight.

The children left their bicycles by the door and went into the dank and dusty ticket office. Old newspapers and sundry wrappings lay in the corner. The window frame hung from one remaining hinge. Flies, brittle in death, littered the windowsill.

209

Shoko left her house and followed the children into the ticket office. She leaned over the counter and said to Liam.

'What are you doing here? I know you, don't I? My daughter Gladys works for your father.'

'Where is Oparee, the bus driver?' Liam asked.

'How should I know?'

Liam hesitated. Should they go back, they had never been on their own before.

'Well, what are you gaping at?'

Jack whispered as he nudged Liam. 'Buy the tickets.'

'Give me three tickets for The Junction,' said Liam, returning his brother's nudge with a slight kick on the shins.

Shoko eyed the note in Liam's hand. She opened a drawer under the counter took out three red tickets. She held them out to Liam. He passed over the five-pound note, Marion's bribe.

'This is not enough,' said the woman taking the money.

'I haven't any more. It cost only three pounds, the price is on the door.'

'That's the old price. I want your bicycles.' She leaned closer to the children.

'No! Give me my money back.'

Shoko let out a roar of laughter. Her drooping breasts wobbled.

Emma began to cry. Liam grabbed the tickets, turned and pushed Jack and his sister out of the office. At the door he stamped on the wheel of his cycle, breaking the spokes. Shoko yelled and shook her fists at him.

The three children squeezed into two seats on the crowded bus as the driver started the engine. The gears grated and black smoke puffed from the exhaust as the lumbering monster inched its way out of the marketplace.

'How far must we go, William?' Jack asked, his voice soft and pleading.

'It's a long way. Give Emma some bread, then go to sleep. The time will go quickly then.'

Jack wriggled Our Haggerty into a comfortable position and closed his eyes.

210

Six hours later the bus jerked to a halt.

'We are at The Junction. You must get off,' the driver told Liam.

Emma began to wail. 'I want to go home.'

'We can't,' said Jack. 'Come, we must get out. Maybe Uncle Seth will be here.'

Stiff and dusty from the long journey the children climbed listlessly from the bus. They stood in the shade against the wall of the trading store – a sad and frightened little group. Their heads turned to watch a blue van pull up. Liam hoped it might be Uncle Seth but two strangers got out.

'Pete, what's that crowd doing there?' asked the shorter of the two and pointed to a group of natives.

'I don't know, boetie.' The second man answered and then saw the children. 'What the h . . . dickens are ya kids doing 'ere?'

The children in unison looked up at the mobile face. They saw a head of frizzy ginger hair nodding at them.

'Waiting for Uncle Seth,' said Jack.

First the nose twitched, followed by a frown then a smile spread over the face. 'Who's Uncle Seth?'

'He's a farmer, also looks for gold,' explained Jack.

'What's your name?'

'I'm Jack, this is my brother and my sister.'

'What's your last name?'

'Auston-Jones,' said Liam.

Emma pulled at the man's trouser leg, he tried to shake her off but she persisted. He looked down at the face, now sticky from the gooseberry jam. 'We're parcels,' she said.

'Yes. Okay kid, you're a parcel. Auston-Jones, Auston-Jones, I know that name.' Pete scratched at his head. 'That fellow, I gave him a lift. Nar, she said she didn't have kids. Ben,' he shouted back into the trading store.

'Yes, Pete,' the shop assistant answered.

'Do you know a farmer called Seth?'

Ben pursed his lips, frowned in thought. 'No. I don't think so.'

Emma pulled at Pete's trouser leg again.

211

He bent his head and asked impatiently, 'Ya, what's you want now?'

'Uncle Seth got red hair,' she told him.

'Oh that's Bwana Carver. Farms about forty miles up the North Road,' explained Ben. 'He was in two days ago. Tried to phone Ashvale.'

Slow clapping interrupted Ben's explanations. The applauding came from the group of natives as a car pulled up. Whispering slithered through the throng, 'M'kama, M'kama,' as the car stopped.

Ben joined them outside the shop and watched as Isaac stepped from the driver's seat. He adjusted his sunglasses and straightened his tie. The natives ignored him. A person quickly slipped to the rear door and opened it. M'kama climbed out and stood facing his followers. He held his spear upright against his side. A fresh leopard skin lay across his shoulder. The whispering increased to a cheer of warm welcome.

M'kama stepped forward and raised his spear in acknowledgement. He smiled at a woman close by. As she approached him, he bowed slightly. M'kama touched her outstretched hand and greeted her. The clapping continued as each person rose to welcome him. They bowed in respect as he greeted them by name.

'That's the famous hunter and storyteller,' said Ben, 'he's honoured in this area. He tells a story of how he rescued a river god years ago. Took her back to the sacred msasa tree. I don't remember the true story. I believe he is returning to his village. The driver is his son Isaac, self-proclaimed chief. He's most unpopular in this area.'

'Well, what do we do with these kids?' said Pete coming back to the immediate problem. 'Do you know when their uncle will be in again?'

Ben shrugged. 'Maybe not for days.'

'We're in a hurry. Have to be in town by two, can't leave them here.' Pete twitched his nose, pulled at his ear as he considered the problem.

'Ask Isaac, he can drop them off at the Bwana Carver's turn-off,' suggested Ben. 'I'll phone him to fetch them.'

Pete looked dubiously at Isaac and shook his head. 'I'm not so sure . . .'

'Don't worry, the old man will take care of them. I know him well. He'll watch out for the kids. Pay Isaac for the petrol,' Ben said, 'while I wash this kid's face.' He took Emma by the hand and disappeared into the store.

Pete approached Isaac with his dilemma. After giving him five notes, Isaac nodded indifferently.

Pete spoke to Liam: 'That man will drop you off at your Uncle's turn-off. Don't worry, your uncle will be there to meet you.'

Liam and Emma sat at the back of the car with M'kama. On the way he pointed out the broken telephone poles. He mimed the action of an elephant rubbing its backside on the poles.

At the wheel, Isaac stretched his arm and grabbed Our Haggerty. Something in the bear's clothing pierced his hand.

'Give it back to me,' yelled the boy.

M'kama cuffed Isaac on the head. 'You may become a leader of our nation, but not by stealing from children.'

Isaac thumped the steering wheel with the palm of his hand. How he wished to be rid of this meddlesome father!

M'kama was asleep when they arrived at the turn-off.

'Get out,' Isaac said and pointed to a dusty track. The children scrambled out of the car.

Alone and forlorn on the dusty road, they watched the car recede over the hill. An eagle circled overhead and bush noises came from the tall grass.

'How can that man phone Uncle Seth if the elephants have knocked the poles over?' reasoned Jack.

Liam gulped his tears back; he wanted to be strong for his brother and sister.

'He can't. We better start walking. Come.' He took Emma by the hand. Following Jack, they started down the rough road.

Little Emma grew weary so Liam carried her. They trudged

on in the heat of the afternoon. Tall grass wavered at the side of the road.

'There's something in the grass. It's coming for us,' Jack whispered.

Liam put Emma down and stood protecting her and Jack. 'What can it be?'

Rustling sounds followed. They grew louder and louder until old Leena stepped onto the road carrying a plastic container filled with water. She wore a blue floral skirt and red blouse. The silk scarf that covered her head had faded. Once the material had been indigo, like the seventh colour of the rainbow.

The children formed a close-knit group as she passed. Keeping to her side of the road, she peered into their faces. She paused in her stride for a moment and pointed to the gap in the grass and then without another glance, she padded on. With the steady rhythm of a heartbeat – the heartbeat of Africa, her footsteps faded into the distance.

The path through the grass ended at a clearing. Liam almost tripped over the rusted parts of a car engine. Close by, a twisted cab lay among weeds and wild marigolds. Beyond a garden patch, a truck with its hood up faced them. A pair of legs stuck out from under a truck. The children watched as a hand appeared. Fingers searched for the screwdriver lying close by. They came closer to an oil can. The next moment a red-headed man pushed himself from under the car as the oil can slipped and spilled over the front of his overall. Emma and Jack let out a peal of laughter. Seth stood up. His jaw dropped.

'What . . . How did you children get here?'

As Emma ran to Seth, William's medals, awarded for bravery fell into the dust. She ran into Seth's arms. He hugged her, then threw her on to a bale of hay.

Jack followed.

'Look, Uncle Seth. Look what Our Haggerty has.' He held up the teddy bear. 'Look in the pocket of her petticoat.'

Seth put his fingers in the small pocket and drew out Hattie's diamond brooch.

214

'Dear God! What's this all about?'

Liam stood at the bottom of the yard and watched Seth toss Jack onto the hay. At last Liam could feel the luxury of tears. He had fulfilled his promise. His brother could laugh again. Seth walked up to the lad and took his hands. Between sobs, Liam tried to tell Seth what had happened.

'They . . . she wants to hurt us, she cut down our tree and filled in the frog pond. They've taken everything. What will we do, Uncle Seth?'

'We find another home, another place to live.' Seth raised the little face and looked into the boy's eyes. In those tears he saw the memories of long ago. He remembered the old Ford standing by the path, and wild marigolds bending in the evening breeze. He heard the emerald-spotted dove's soft call and saw the touch of sunset in the clouds. The voice of a child came back to him as she ran down the path: 'I'm here, Seth, I'm safe.'

'Hattie, Hattie, I didn't stay to help you,' Seth whispered. 'I won't let you down again, I'll take care of your children.'

He held the boy close to his heart and turned to watch Jack. The small boy was jumping up and down and throwing handfuls of hay above his head. His laughter echoed through the woodlands.

Epilogue

In 1964 a doctor hung a watercolour in his English country home. The picture was titled *Frith* and it showed a little boy leading a span of oxen and a covered wagon. Amethyst hills and a msasa tree rose in the distance. The picture was signed, W A-J 1936, and it was the artist's only surviving work.

A note attached behind the frame read, 'From Emma, with thanks.'